HARDWAY

HARDWAY

BY HECTOR ACOSTA

HARDWAY

A NOVELLA

HECTOR ACOSTA

Published by **Shotgun Honey Books**

215 Loma Road
Charleston, WV 25314
www.ShotgunHoney.com

Cover Design by Bad Fido.

ISBN-10: 1-956957-38-3
ISBN-13: 978-1-956957-38-9

10 9 8 7 6 5 4 3 2   24 23 22 21 20 19 18

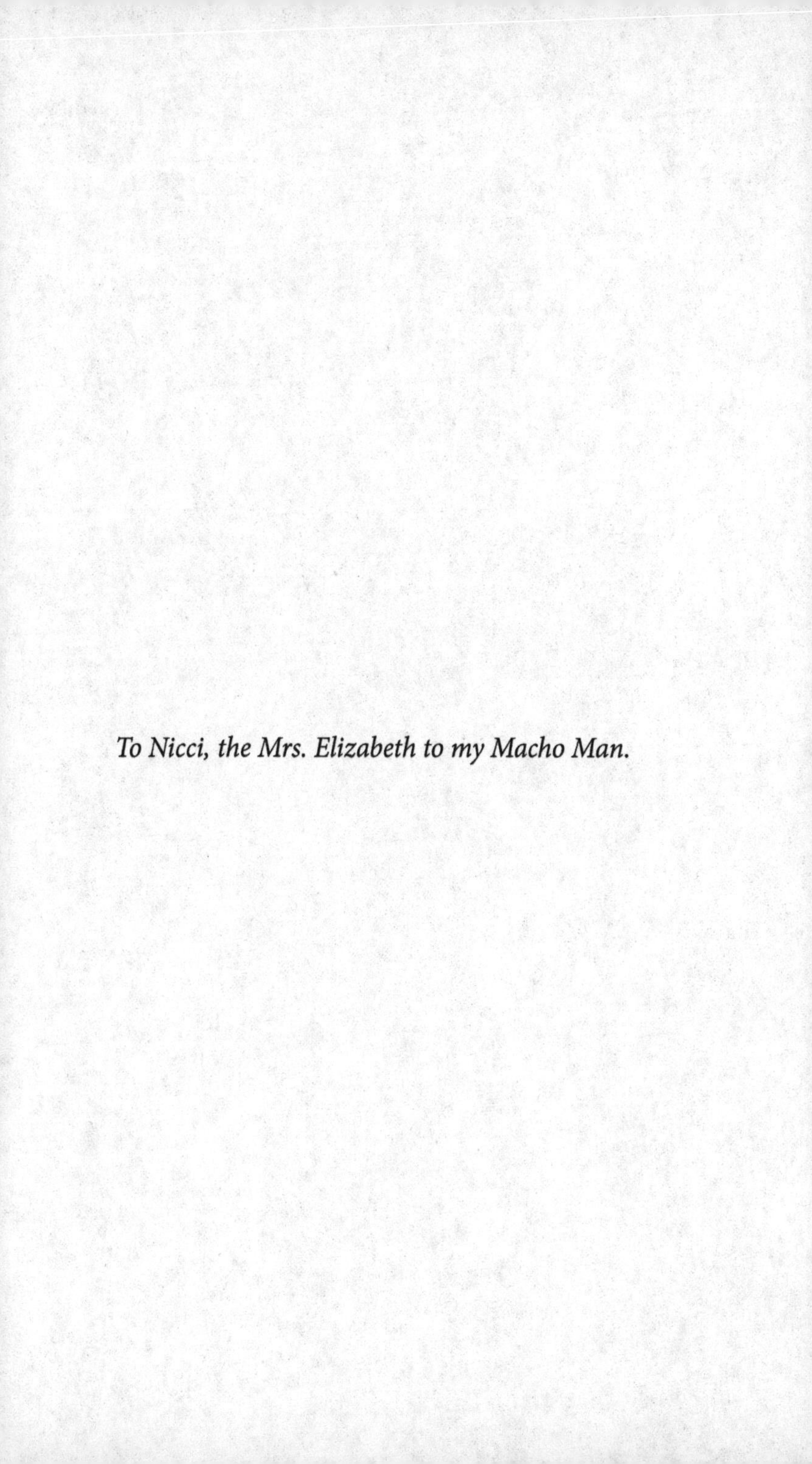

To Nicci, the Mrs. Elizabeth to my Macho Man.

HARDWAY

CHAPTER ONE

 grab a fluorescent bulb and bring it down on Carlos' shaved head. He opens the small, black notebook lying on his lap and in neat letters writes *light bulbs*. Looking up, he's just in time to see Carlos take a second shot to the head. The long glass tube explodes in the same manner Spencer imagines stars do, in a singular, stunning moment of transformation leaving only streaming, white powder behind.

The kids and unemployed adults making up most of the day's crowd ooh at the sight of Carlos staggering around with glass sticking out of his head. Spencer smiles. Everyone loves a good light bulb shot. Probably the only thing they like more is the sight of a table on fire.

He adds lighter fluid to the list of items to buy.

The match takes place in a small, grassy area between two apartment buildings. A chain link fence separates the

1

buildings and an empty lot. Along the walls rest an armory of dollar store weapons, including a couple of cheap pots and pans, an aluminum tray, and a scratched up stop sign. Lightbulbs like the one James used on Carlos litter the ground.

Picking the glass from his head, Carlos rolls his neck and rushes James. Everyone can see it's a stupid thing to do, because while James might be a skinny, fifteen-year-old with a mullet and pimples all over his face, he's also holding a large aluminum tray in his hands. Even Carlos thought it was a stupid move when Spencer first told him the finish to the match.

"That's the point," Spencer said back when was laying out the match on his kitchen table. "You're Carlos the Bull and you don't think anything can hurt you."

"Fuck yeah nothing can hurt me."

"No, see, you *think* nothing can hurt you. That's why even though you just took a shot to the head, you're still rushing James. Cause of hubris."

"Hu-whatt?"

"Hubris," Spencer repeated, spending the next five minutes explaining to the three-hundred pound eighteen-year-old what hubris meant. At the end, Carlos shrugged and asked only one question;

"Can it be two shots to the head? You know, make me look really badass."

Two shots to the head it is. Spencer winces in sympathy at the loud crack the tray makes when it connects with Carlos' skull. The big Mexican sways left and right, a glazed look on his face. He oversells a bit too much for Spencer's liking, and finally crashes face first to the blue mat. James wastes no time throwing himself on top.

One.

Two.

Three.

Spencer is so busy writing down the results he almost forgets the next part. Getting up from the grass, he steps over a bent whiffle bat and raises James's hand.

"The winner, and number one contender for the Royal Brooks Apartments Wrestling League is James 'The Innovator' Henricks!"

The crowd pays no attention. Most are already walking away, and the few who remain are scrolling down on their phones and talking among each other.

"Don't forget to come back in a month for our big show! All the titles will be on the line!" Spencer shouts.

"Is it just me, or are the crowds getting smaller?" Carlos asks, picking glass from his head.

"It's those Woodland Terrace assholes. I heard they were putting on a show today as well," James says.

Carlos makes a face. "Douchebags. First, they steal our wrestlers, and now they steal RBWL's crowd."

"Wait," Spencer interrupts, "What are you talking about?"

"Haven't you heard?" Carlos asks, "Mikey's family got evicted last week. They're moving over to Woodland Terrace."

"So? That doesn't mean he's going to start wrestling for them."

"He ain't walking a mile back and forth for every show. Not when there's a wrestling promotion already set up in his new backyard. I hear they even got a ring over there. Apartment manager doesn't say shit about it," he tells James.

"Yeah?"

"Yeah. Plus, they're paying their guys."

"Bullshit."

Carlos plucks a large piece of glass from his arm. "That's what I heard." Holding the glass between his fingers, he shows it to James and Spencer, "ECdub or what?" he says, referring to the nickname given to the televised wrestling promotion notorious for their liberal use of weapons and blood.

"Nice," James says.

Spencer barely notices. He's too busy trying to figure out how losing Mikey will affect their upcoming show.

"Hey Spencer, I told you I want to change my name, right?" James asks. "Thinking of going by Dementor now."

"Uh," Spencer mutters, flipping through the pages on his notebook. "You're going on vacation next month, right? Let's wait until after you come back from that. Build it up."

Jaimie nods. "That'll work. Gives me time to bulk up and look all ripped," he says, rolling up the sleeves of his tattered Iron Maiden shirt and flexing.

"So gay," Carlos says.

"Your face is gay," James replies.

Carlos hits James on the shoulder and says, "Come on, I'm hungry. Let's go get some Taco Cabana."

"Man, you just ate there yesterday."

"That was Taco Bell. Big difference."

Already they're walking away. Neither bothers to say goodbye to Spencer.

Putting his notebook in his back pocket, Spencer begins to clean up. He drags the wrestling mats and blankets to the old shed on the other side of the Dallas apartment complex and afterwards sweeps the area for stray glass. Spencer has done this after every show, just like he promised the apartment manager he would. This and twenty dollars a month lets the manager turn a blind eye on their shows.

By the time Spencer's done climbing the steps to his family's third story apartment, he's sweaty, tired, and hungry. He finds the door to their apartment unlocked. Either his older brother is home, or their dad forgot to lock it on his way out to his job at the call center.

Billy doesn't acknowledge Spencer when he steps inside their small, two-bedroom apartment. Spencer's older brother is sitting on their beat-up sofa next to a pretty, dark skin girl. When Spencer walks in, Billy's working to unhook the girl's bra.

It's the girl who notices Spencer standing by the doorway. Pushing Billy away, she covers her chest and smiles.

"Hey, Spence."

Spencer waves an awkward hello. "Hey, Tori." The snapshot of Tori in her black bra presses on his mind, and he can feel other things below his waist pressing against the fabric of his jeans. "How are you?"

"She'd be better if you hadn't interrupted," Billy mutters.

"Don't listen to Billy," Tori says, punching Spencer's seventeen-year-old brother on the shoulder. To the disappointment of Spencer, she slips back into her shirt and asks, "How today go?"

The image of Tori leaves Spencer's mind, replaced by the events of just a couple of hours ago. He tells her about the show and she listens to it all, nodding and laughing at just the right moments. She even claps when he tells her how James won against Carlos.

This makes Spencer love her even more.

"Couldn't have gone that well. The champ wasn't there," Billy says. He jumps up from the couch and walks over to their kitchen, opening up cabinets and looking through the pile of dishes on the sink before settling on a cup which he runs through the faucet.

Familiar pangs of jealousy and betrayal creep up Spencer's spine like tiny spiders as he watches his brother open the refrigerator door and pour himself some juice. Last year, right around the time their mother left them, his brother discovered their father's old weight set. It didn't take long before Billy was skipping out on their usual Friday nights of eating burgers and playing videogames, preferring instead to spend his time with newfound friends and chasing after girls.

At least they still had wrestling. Spencer can still remember sitting cross-legged next to Billy on the carpet of their parent's old bedroom, staring in awe at the television and watching giants trek across a blood-stained ring, punching each other for the approval of the crowd. His father would occasionally chime in and name whatever move the wrestlers did, while their mother rolled her eyes and reminded him for the hundredth time how Billy and Spencer were too young to watch so much violence. This was before she became sullen and closed off to the world, long before she packed up and left.

It was also before their father's company got outsourced to India and he had to start working at the new call center. Before Billy shed sixty pounds, joined the football team, and started to ignore Spencer any time they crossed each other in the school's hallways. Before they moved from their old house and into the Royal Brooks Apartment complex.

"Where were you? Spencer asks Billy.

Tossing a can of soda to Tori, Billy says, "Out. I had something to do."

"You were supposed to be there." Spencer immediately wishes he could swallow the words back. He sounds so childish.

"Hey, even the wrestling champ needs a day off every now and then. Ain't that right, Tori?"

Tori leans over the couch. "I knew you could run things, Spencer." Her accompanying wink dries Spencer's mouth and whisks away all thoughts from his head. She turns to Billy, "You think we should tell him?"

"No," Billy says with a crushing simplicity.

"Tell me what?" Spencer asks.

"Don't worry about it. Trust me, it's better that I didn't show up today. I can't be giving this," Billy sets his glass down and fondles his chest, "away at every show, man.

Ain't that right, Tori?"

"We really had something important to do," Tori says.

"And we still do," Billy pushes Spencer aside and walks

back to the couch. "So why don't you go to our room and not come back for an hour?"

"Make it two, yeah, Spence?" Tori asks, already leaning back on the couch and taking off her shirt.

Spencer stiffly walks into his room and shuts the door behind him. He grabs the fantasy book he checked out of the library and lies on his bed. The story of the witty and scarred mercenary hired to kill a king's daughter doesn't hold his attention for long. After spending ten minutes on the same page, Spencer throws the book on the floor and stares up at the ceiling. He thinks about the upcoming Royal Brooks Wrestling show, the first scheduled to be recorded using a video camera he found at a garage sale last month. It needs to be good. Maybe after he films it he can go over to the school's computer lab and see if they can help him edit it. Put it up on web like all the other videos he's seen.

It isn't long before the sounds of the living room push through and fill the small bedroom. Spencer considers reaching for his headphones, but Tori's muffled laugh, dripping with an excitement he desperately wishes was directed at him stops him. Closing his eyes, he brings back the image of her in her bra. He waits until her moans become louder and faster before wiggling out of his pants and touching himself. He tries to match their rhythm.

He fails, lasting only a few minutes before all the tension he's been holding onto releases into his sheets. Drenched in sweat and shame, he kicks the sheets off his bed, takes off his shirt, and tries to go to sleep.

CHAPTER TWO

SOCIAL DISTORTION EXPLODES into the room, Mike Ness' guitar gnawing on Spencer's sleep while the singer implores him to reach for the sky. Instead, Spencer puts a pillow over his head. It does very little to drown out the music or his older brother singing along with it.

"Can't you take a day off?" Spencer shouts after a few minutes.

"What?"

Spencer throws the pillow against the wall and turns to look at his brother.

Wearing only a pair of boxer shorts, Billy sits on the edge of his bed, a set of weights in his hands. The beat-up stereo on the dresser next to him blares out a new song Spencer doesn't recognize. Again, Spencer is reminded how much his brother has changed. Growing up, everyone used to comment how much the two of them looked alike despite their two year difference in age. Same greasy, unkempt brown hair, same pale, blotchy skin, and same sharp brown eyes. For good or bad, Spencer still retains most of those qualities, but Billy dropped them like he dropped Advanced Calculus in school. Now his hair is nicely kept, and his skin has taken a healthy tan thanks to daily football practice during the school year.

"It's Sunday. Can't you lay off the exercise for one day?"

Setting the weights down on the floor, Billy reaches for the towel on the dresser and wipes the sweat off his face.

"I said…"

Billy raises a hand and uses his other one to beat on an invisible drum kit. When the song finishes, he reaches over to the stereo and clicks it off. "What were you saying?" Billy asks.

"Nothing," Spencer says and closes his eyes.

"Hey Spencer."

"I'm sleeping."

"No, you're not."

"I'm trying to."

"Yeah, well, not hard enough. Anyways, this is important."

"What?" Spencer opens his eyes and finds the bed sheets from last night hovering above him like a ghost who doesn't know how cliché he's being.

"If you're going to splooge all over your bed sheets, can you at least keep them on your side of the room?" Billy asks, dropping the sheet on Spencer's face. "Seriously, dude, we share a room. Do it in the shower like normal people."

Spencer recoils when the sheet touches his face, clawing at it until he gets it off and kicks it to the edge of his bed, where it lays like a rumpled one night stand. He checks his clock. It's not even eight in the morning yet. "Can I go back to sleep now?"

"No. Come on, it's time for you to get up." Billy shakes the bed. "Come on, get up."

Groaning, Spencer folds his arms across his chest and refuses to move until Billy leans close and whispers, "Tori is making us breakfast. Eggs, bacon, pancakes, the whole shebang. I'm surprised your snout hasn't smelled it yet." He pinches Spencer's nose and jumps back before Spencer can swat him away.

Pushing himself up from the bed, Spencer asks, "Tori's here?"

"Yep," Billy answers, already moving towards the door. "Hurry up and come out when you're decent." He leaves, only to pop his head back into the room and give Spencer a serious look. "You know, if you got up with me and did some exercise in the morning, you could lose some weight. Then you would just need to stop reading so much and not be such a pussy about talking to girls to put an end to," he makes a general motion in Spencer's direction, "all this."

Yawning, Spencer spends a few more minutes in bed. As usual, his brain is filled with retorts to Billy's words, all of them coming too late to actually be said aloud. He stores them in the back of his head, in a file drawer overstuffed with words he's never uttered and actions he's never taken. Finding the jeans he wore yesterday and a shirt which only smells two days old, he looks around. Sharing a room is still new to both brothers. Back in better days—Spencer's definition of 'better days' is in constant flux, but today it means when they lived in their old house—each brother had a room of their own.

In the beginning it hadn't been too bad, but as Billy changed, so did his side of the room. The wrestling posters went down, replaced with a corkboard full of pictures of all his new friends and Tori. Their dad's weight set now stood by the corner of his room, having replaced the television set which had been moved to the living room, despite Spencer's protests.

At least Spencer has his bookshelf. It's one of the few things they brought with them from the old house, with the rest of their stuff either sold off or in a storage unit neither brother is sure their father still pays for. Spencer occasionally finds himself staring at the books lining the shelves and wondering what the point of holding on to them is.

When he walks out of the room, Spencer finds Tori in the kitchen.

"You want some eggs?" she asks.

"Yeah, thanks."

Billy's already sitting at their kitchen table, a glass full of the thick green liquid he drinks every morning in front of him. Spencer tried it once and thought it tasted like a combination of mildew and sweat.

Tori sings as she cooks. It's a loud, out of tune version of a song that's been playing in all the radio stations, and somehow she still manages to get most of the words wrong. But the way she moves her body as she sings, swaying left and right and throwing her head back to belt out the really loud parts makes up for the bad singing. She's wearing the same shirt she had on yesterday, meaning she probably slept over. When she brings out the plate piled high with scrambled eggs and thick slices of bacon, Spencer realizes she's wearing little else. Color rises up to his cheeks as he stares at her long, muscular legs and black panties matching the bra from yesterday.

If either Tori or Billy notice his discomfort, they don't say anything.

"Plans for today?" Tori asks, heading back to the kitchen and flipping over the pancakes.

"Probably just hang around the house."

"Oh no, you're not doing that," Billy says, gulping down the rest of his protein shake and wiping his mouth. "I've seen what you do when you 'hang around'. Before long we'll need to burn all the sheets in the house." Spencer's face turns red.

Tori continues to hum in the kitchen. "Dig in guys, pancakes will be done soon. Hey, Billy, I'm going to make some for your dad too, okay?"

"Dad's not here?" Spencer asks.

"Working another double," Billy says.

"That's the second one this week."

"Third. But I think he'll be able to stop working so much soon. I got a job."

Spencer stops, his fork halfway to his mouth. "You did? How? I thought Dad didn't want you to work. Where? How?"

Before Billy can answer, Tori places a plate stacked high with packages in the center of the table. With a flourish, she steps back and takes a bow, saying "Gentlemen, breakfast is served."

They all pile pancakes on their plates and start eating. For a few minutes, there are no words spoken other than Spencer asking to pass the ketchup. The eggs are fluffy, the bacon crisp, and the pancakes contain hints of cinnamon. Spencer didn't even know they had cinnamon. Finishing his eggs, Spencer can no longer stand it and blurts out, "Well? Where are you going to be working? For how much? When do you start?"

Billy looks up from his plate. "Dude, rude. You could at least thank Tori for the breakfast first."

"Thanks, Tori," Spencer says.

She smiles and pats his hand, sending a jolt of pleasure through his body, "He's just teasing you. And getting ahead of himself. What your brother meant to say was that he applied for a job. Jobs actually. That's what we were doing yesterday. Going around applying at places."

"Oh," Spencer says, somewhat deflated. Billy getting a job would have been good news, not only because of the extra income, but also because it would mean he wouldn't be around the house as much. And maybe Tori would get bored and still drop by. Spencer reigns in his thoughts before they can get too far on what could happen with a bored Tori and Spencer in a house all to themselves.

"I'm getting a job," Billy says in between stuffing eggs into his mouth. "Just a matter of time. Remember the guy at Dairy Queen? He was practically offering me the job on the spot."

"He said they were interviewing people next week," Tori says.

"Same thing."

"What about Dad?"

"He's just going to have to live with it. I'm like the only guy I know who doesn't have a job."

Billy and Spencer's father had refused to hear any talk about Billy getting a job. "Enjoy your last summer before graduating high school," he told Billy.

"Wait," Spencer says, "If you get a job, what's going to happen to RBWL?" RBWL stood for their backyard wrestling promotion—The Royal Brooks Wrestling League.

Billy shrugs. "I dunno. You can get someone else to be your champion, I guess."

Spencer's mouth goes dry and he stares down at his plate, having lost his appetite. Anger presses against his stomach and makes the eggs he just ate dance their way up to his throat. *This isn't fair*, he thinks. It's not just the idea of losing Billy as a champion which bothers him.

Billy stepping away from their wrestling league would sever whatever little connection was left of the brother's old relationship.

Shifting in his chair, the food rolls around his stomach. Billy looking for a job feels like a giant betrayal. Like his tag team partner just brought a chair down on his back.

CHAPTER THREE

GRABBING HIS NOTEBOOK and wallet from the bedroom, Spencer exits the apartment. A wall of heat waits for him outside, and by the time he reaches the ground floor, his shirt is clinging to him like an adoring fan, beads of sweat pooling around the pockets of fat between his chest and torso.

Parched and already regretting his decision of leaving the apartment, Spencer starts walking towards the front gate. His plan is to catch the nearby bus and go to the dollar movies. He isn't sure what's playing there today, but at least it'll be cool inside the theater, and maybe a movie will keep his mind off the conversation he just had with Billy.

The Royal Brook's Apartments are just one of many complexes lining the North Dallas neighborhood they live in. All of the complexes share the same stucco building design, with sloping, half cut grass hills, and names meant to invoke a classier living than onsite laundromats and roach infested kitchens. Their dad chose Royal Brooks after weighing the cost of the apartment versus the chances of having his boys get robbed by a meth addict. They'd originally intended to move to the apartments across the street but those plans were laid by the wayside when they drove past it one day and saw the eight squad cars in the parking lot.

A drug deal gone bad the newspapers told them the next day. "Must have gone really bad," their dad said, throwing the half-filled application in the trash.

In the year of living in Royal Brook's, the worse any of them had seen were a couple of drunken fights, most ending as quickly as they began. Cops occasionally were spotted patrolling the area, but Spencer never saw them do anything other than park their squad cars and drink from their Big Gulps. This was not necessarily a bad thing. Spencer imagines a more studious cop would have questions as to why some of the younger Royal Brooks tenants seem to have new injuries every other week.

So far Billy and Spencer have managed to avoid their father finding out about the wrestling league through a combination of a grueling work schedule on their dad's side, make-up (carefully applied by Tori), and general avoidance, which their dad probably attributed to teenage moodiness.

"Hey, Spencer, yo, wait up!"

Spencer turns and sees Carlos running down the hill after him. When he reaches Spencer, Carlos' face is a mask of red, the sounds coming out of his mouth resembling a freight train going off the rails.

The pounds of shame Spencer carries with him momentarily lessen when faced with someone more out of shape than himself. But they're packed back in the moment Carlos straightens up and towers over him. Spencer considers Carlos *lucky fat*, able to carry his girth and be imposing, rather than insignificant.

"You've seen your brother, dude?" Carlos asks in between gulps of air.

"Last I saw him, he and Tori were in our apartment."

"Shit. Your apartment, yeah, I should have checked there first."

Carlos is about to take off in the direction he came from when Spencer stops him. "Hey, why are you looking for my brother?"

"I wanted to show him this," Carlos says, unfolding a piece of paper.

"Where'd you find this?"

"Stuck to my door. There's a shit-ton of them plastered on the buildings by the entrance. I got James and some of the other guys taking them down. That's some fucked up shit, right?"

It is. What Spencer holds in his hand is a flyer for WTF— The Woodland Terrace Federation. It bothers Spencer to see the lack of the word wrestling anywhere in the title. The flyer is made of a glossy paper stock, the type Spencer knows you have to go to a copy store to get made. And it's in color to boot.

It shows a collage of teenagers playing at being wrestlers. Some are bared chested, others have ripped t-shirts, and there's even two in cheap lucha masks, like the type Mexican wrestlers often wear in the ring. Most are frozen in poses which they'd probably imagined looked intimidating or impressive, but in Spencer's eyes, only make them look constipated. In the center there's a picture of a skinny guy with a limp green mohawk leaning slightly to the right. He's staring ahead with a seriousness which loops right around and becomes almost comical.

Spencer would find all this a lot funnier if it wasn't for the fact the flyer is still worlds better than anything the RBWL has managed to ever produce. He stares at the paper, the desire to rip it in two tickling Spencer's fingers and making him dizzy.

It isn't fair, he thinks for the second time this morning.

"Look dude," Carlos says, jabbing his fat brown finger at the flyer and drawing Spencer's eyes down to the bottom, where he reads the following

EDDIE TORNADO

VS

JAMES 'HIGH ROLLER' HAYES

FOR THE

WTF CHAMPIONSHIP

"They're calling us out," Carlos says, pointing to the last line. "Fuckers saying we're not, like real wrestling and stuff. I bet they don't even know about hubris like we do."

Spencer folds up the flyer and sticks it in between the pages of his notebook. He's reminded of the story they read in English class last year about the guy who murders an old man and sticks him under the floorboards. Just like the narrator in the story could hear the murdered heart, Spencer can still see the flyer in his mind, the words beating red like the heart in the story must have.

"Hey, Carlos, can you do me a favor?"

"What up?"

"Don't show this to Billy, yet. Just go back and make sure to get all the flyers."

Carlos gives him the same look he did when Spencer tried to explain hubris to him. "You sure, man? I mean, I know you like to run RBWL, but like, Billy is probably the guy to go with this. I bet he can think of some way of getting back at them. You know he hates Eddie."

Spencer nods and resists the urge to swat away the words from the flyer, still dancing on the edge of his vision. "Which is why you gotta let me tell him. I don't want him doing something stupid."

Carlos pounds his fists together and says, "He wouldn't be alone, you get me?"

Another nod. "Yeah, I know. But just let me do it, okay?"

The large Mexican stares at Spencer and chews on his lower lip, which Spencer can't decide if it's because he's in deep thought or just hungry. "Alright, man. But you guys better come up with something quick. We don't want to look like pussies, right?"

"We don't," Spencer says.

CHAPTER FOUR

IT'S HARD TO SAY who initially came up with the idea of starting a wrestling promotion. If you believed Billy, it was their idea first, hatched after a night of watching wrestling and Billy complaining the wresters were all out of shape has-beens. This was followed up by Spencer muttering how he'd like to see his brother do better.

It was a remark Spencer forgot about almost immediately, but the comment must have stayed with Billy, because a couple of days later he'd rounded up a group of kids from around the apartment complex, all interested in learning more about how they could hit each other with chairs and aluminum pans and become famous for it. Spencer originally balked at joining, but Billy's insistence coupled with the promise he could write the storylines, got him to agree. A couple of days later, the pretty black girl from across the building knocked on their door and said she wanted to be a wrestler too.

By the time they were ready to put on their first show, the rumors of another promotion starting up nearby were well known. "Fucking copycats," Billy told the group as they sat around their living room and discussed their upcoming matches. Spencer hadn't understood why his brother was so annoyed at hearing about Woodland Terrace. In his view, this was a good thing. Already he had multiple inter-promotional storylines written down in his notebook, and couldn't wait to share it with the Woodland Terrace guys.

However, things like the flyer made it clear Woodland Terrace has no intentions of playing nice with Royal Brooks. This sits just fine with guys like Billy and Carlos, who already take Woodland Terrace's presence as an insult needing to be addressed, but worries Spencer. It's why he didn't go straight to Billy with the flyer. Ever since he lost the weight and gained friends, Billy has taken to walking around with an impulsiveness fitting him tighter than a lucky pair of underwear. True, the impulsiveness has led to some interesting things, such as the creation of RBWL, but Spencer can't help but continue to worry. He's seen enough wrestling to know false bravado when it is sitting in the living room couch next to him.

Spencer ends up watching a silly comedy which isn't funny enough to get his mind off Woodland Terrace. Stepping out of the theater, he checks the movie board and sees nothing of interest immediately playing, so he walks over to the arcade machines by the far end of the theater to kill some time. Skipping over the stained Pac-Man cabinet and the bleating pinball machine based on a failed movie license, he settles on the fighting game he plays whenever he comes here. Rolling a quarter into the cabinet's slot, Spencer moves the joystick around to get a feel of how sticky it is and chooses his usual fighter.

He becomes so invested in landing a ten-hit combo on his computer opponent he doesn't notice the person standing next to him until he catches the flickering image of a green mohawk—bowing slightly to the right—reflected on the dusty screen.

The sight almost costs Spencer the match, but at the last minute he's able to counter his opponent's super move with a combination of harsh flicks of the joystick and sheer luck. The win still looks impressive. "Not bad," Eddie Tornado says, the thick Southern drawl sounding strange coming out of his pierced lips. He's wearing a jean jacket adorned with multiple patches of band's logos and stands with his hands in his pocket, an easy confidence unspooling from his skinny frame.

Spencer doesn't say anything and just waits for the next match to load.

Eddie slides a quarter into the coin slot and presses down on the faded second player button. "You don't mind, right?" he asks Spencer, stepping forward to grab the joystick.

"No," Spencer says as they return to the fighter select screen. He sticks to the same fighter he's been using and watches Eddie's blinking cursor move from fighter to fighter before ending on a buxom woman.

"I get a kick of seeing them bounce," Eddie says by way of explanation.

Their match is over quick, Spencer making such short work of Eddie he surprises even himself.

"Fuck, that right there demands a rematch. What you say?"

Spencer nods his head, never turning away from the arcade screen. He's trying to figure out if Eddie knows who he is.

This time Eddie picks a big, but slow moving fighter. The match takes longer than before, but Spencer still comes out winning.

"Goddamn, fucking thing must be busted," Eddie says, swatting his joystick. "I bet if I was on your side I could win."

Before he can help it, Spencer asks, "Want to switch?"

Eddie pushes his mohawk back and eyes him, "Yeah, let's do that." He places yet another quarter into the machine.

Both teens select the same fighters from their first match. True to his word, Eddie plays better on that side, but Spencer is still the superior player, and is close to winning the match when Eddie asks, "You're Billy's brother ain't ya?"

The question catches Spencer off guard and his onscreen fighter pays for it, Eddie landing several punches before Spencer manages to tap the block button and push his fighter away.

"You two don't look nothin' alike, I tell ya." Eddie's fighter moves in, forcing Spencer to remain in a crouching block. "Guess I can see why you remain on the sidelines while he gets the belt." Eddie wiggles his joystick and taps out a Morse code of punches and kicks through the arcade cabinet's buttons. There's a flash on the screen and then Spencer's fighter is on the ground, his entire life bar depleted.

"Not that being the champion of your little rinky-dink promotion is much to crow about," Eddie adds.

Spencer takes a deep breath and hunches down on his side of the cabinet, prompting a laugh out of Eddie. "Look who's gotten all aggro on me. Told you I was a better player on this side."

They start the second round of the match. Spencer tries all the moves which previously worked only to find Eddie can block and counter them all. And in return Spencer is unable to block every other move Eddie does with his character. Spencer gives himself a second to flick his eyes upwards to where his long, rectangular life line is flashing red, an indication he's about to lose the match.

"You guy don't even have a real ring. Ain't no wonder everyone prefers WTF."

Biting his lower lip, Spencer desperately moves the joystick around to move his fighter out of the corner he's been wedged in and tries to block out Eddie's words. He blinks away the sweat from his eyes and tries to focus on his onscreen avatar. The joystick is slippery in his hands and his fingers can't quite seem to hit the button as quickly as he'd like.

"You know what I don't get? Why in the blue hell Tori hangs around with you guys. What does a broke ass boyfriend and his porker of a brother have to offer a fine ass girl like that, huh?"

The words cut through Spencer's defenses as easily as Eddie's avatar breaks through Spencer's fighter and continues the beating. The life bar above his character's head dwindles down and pulses red. The copper taste of blood fills his mouth, having bitten his lip so hard to break the skin. Before he fully realizes what he's doing, Spencer lets go of the joystick and swings his fist in Eddie's direction.

The punch lands awkwardly on Eddie's lower jaw, and isn't even hard enough to get him to release his joystick.

Spencer takes a step back and watches Eddie touch the spot where Spencer's punch landed. He releases his joystick, glances at Spencer. "Big fucking mistake, titty boy."

CHAPTER FIVE

"HERE, TAKE THIS," Carlos says.

Spencer eyes the frozen slice of chicken and shakes his head.

"Come on, it'll bring the swelling down."

"That's steak, dumbass," James says. "All that thing is going to do is give him salmonella."

"Well, it's all I have. Even if I had steak, I wouldn't waste it on him. No offense, Spencer."

Leaning back against the sofa, Spencer goes back to counting the water stains on the ceiling with his one good eye. His left eye stays closed and purple, a pulse of pain living behind his eyelid.

The sofa shifts when Tori sits next to him. "Here you go," she whispers, placing a bag of ice on his eye.

"That fucking motherfucker." Without looking Spencer

knows his brother is pacing back and forth in front of him. "Dude has no idea what he just started."

Spencer closes his right eye and tries to focus on how good the bag of ice feels. He wishes the coldness could numb his brain just like it's doing to the left side of his face. Because the cold can't touch his brain, he's left to think about the beating Eddie gave him. Spencer imagines he didn't get a very severe one—just a black eye and a bruised ass from when Eddie pushed him down to the floor. There's a chance the beating might have continued if it wasn't for the theater manager kicking Eddie out. But the way Eddie left without making a scene, the grin still on his face while he readjusted his mohawk, makes Spencer think the whole thing was just to prove the same point plastering the flyers all around Royal Brooks did.

We're coming for you and there's nothing you can do to stop it.

"We're kicking their ass, right, Billy?" Carlos throws his weight into the end of the sofa. He's still holding the frozen piece of chicken. "This type of shit can't stand. Makes us look like pussies." He punctuates his sentences by jabbing the chicken into the arm of the sofa.

They're in Carlos's apartment, Spencer having decided to come here rather than head straight home. He wasn't sure his dad was scheduled to be off work already, and didn't want to risk having to explain the black eye in the off chance he was. Sarlos lived by himself, his parents and their whereabouts an unknown quantity to everyone. When Carlos saw Spencer, and heard the story of where he got the black eye, he called

James and Billy over, who much to Spencer's embarrassment brought Tori along.

"We don't have to do anything," Spencer says.

"We should interrupt their next show. Just run in and start beating the shit out of them," James says. "It'll be like a hardcore shoot no one sees coming."

"Woah, I mean, I want payback and everything, but I don't think we should be shooting anyone," Carlos says.

"No, dumbass, not shooting. Shoot. You know, when something real happens in the ring. Like when Hart got screwed out of the title by Vince McMahon."

"I still say that was all just part of a storyline," Carlos argues.

"We don't have to do anything," Spencer tries again.

"Bullshit, man. It was all real. No way they could keep a story like that going for years. What would be the point?"

"Guys, I think Spencer is trying to say something," Tori says and touches Spencer's arm. This sends tingles all over his body and causes the usual reaction in his pants. He shifts around in the sofa and tries to focus on unsexy things, like the time he caught his grandma getting out of the shower.

"Hey, can we maybe get back to talking how we're going to deal with those assholes?" Billy interrupts Carlos and James's argument.

Spencer makes himself mentally go through every of his grandma's wrinkle until the tightness in his pant subsides. "Let's just let it go."

He can feel three pair of eyes on him.

"Dude, your brother can be such a pussy," Carlos says.

"Tell me about it," Billy answers. "I like James idea. They

got a show next week, right? Let's just go out there, the three of us, and show them they shouldn't mess with Royal Brooks."

The words are making Spencer's head throb harder than his bruised eye. He rubs his forehead and gets up from the couch. "Since when do you care what happens to RBWL?" Spencer asks his brother. "Weren't you telling me earlier this morning how you were going to vacate the title soon as you found a job?"

"Wait what?" James says.

"Tell them," Spencer says, looking at his brother. "Tell them how you're ready to leave RBWL 'cause you rather be flipping burgers like a tool over at Dairy Queen."

"Shut up, Spencer," Billy says, glaring at him. He turns to James and Carlos and explains, "I got some applications for some places and this dude is all butt-hurt about it."

"You can't have it both ways," Spencer says, "You're madder about the flyers than someone beating up your own brother."

"Come on Spence, that's not true. That's why I want payback."

"You've wanted payback ever since you heard about Woodland Terrace. It just bugs you to know that someone out there is doing the same thing you are, maybe even better, doesn't it? That you're not the special little snowflake you think you are. That's why you treat me like shit sometimes and are cool other times. You can't decide if you're embarrassed of your fat-ass brother, or happy he's a fat ass, so that you can shine even brighter around your friends."

"Awkward," Carlos says in a high falsetto.

Billy steps up to Spencer and jabs him in the chest, "Fuck

you. Don't pin your shit on me, man. I'm not force feeding you Big Macs or begging you to sit your ass in front of the TV."

"Billy…" Tori says.

"Nah, nah, he needs to hear this," Billy continues, his eyes fixed on Spencer. "I'm tired of you blaming everyone and everything anytime shit doesn't go your way. You bitched about RBWL being a stupid idea in the first place, but now? Now you're probably more into it than anyone else, always carrying around that stupid notebook and boring Tori and me with your wrestling talk."

"Shut up," Spencer says. His hands are rolled into fists, nails pressing into his skin and sending bites of pain into his nerve. "Shut up, Billy."

"I bet you blame Dad for Mom leaving, you selfish brat."

After going almost fifteen years without punching someone, Spencer swings his fist for the second time in one day. His punch connects with Billy's stomach, Spencer getting a thrill when he hears the satisfying sound of air escaping his brother's mouth.

"You little asshole," Billy mutters and reaches out for Spencer. He's held back at the last minute by James, who grabs him by the shoulder.

"Dude, chill, man."

"Douche sucker punched me," Billy says, glaring at Spencer with seething anger. .

"Yeah, I saw, but that mom thing was kinda low, dude. Let's all relax. Remember, it's Woodland Terrace who are the real fuckers."

"Plus, you should save all that aggression for the ring. We could pitch it as 'blood vs. blood'," Carlos adds.

Tori steps in between Spencer and Billy and says, "You're not helping, Carlos," before turning to Billy and adding,

"And neither are you."

"He started it," Billy mutters like a child being admonished by a teacher.

"Just," Tori takes a deep breath and raises her hands up, "enough. From everyone. This is getting out hand. Maybe the best thing to do is have RBWL take a break. School is starting up soon, so there's that to think about."

The words slam into Spencer and he feels a pain unlike any before. It reaches his core and swats away whatever defenses he's built up over two years of middle school and one year of high school. Hearing Tori suggest ending RBWL pierces the part of him where all his ideas and day dreams are born from. His nails dig harder into his skin and he rapidly blinks his eyes, the start of tears watering his vision, causing everything around him to become unclear and faded.

"That would suck. We'd be less WWE and more WCW, then," Carlos says, referring to the big national wrestling promotion which went under a couple of years back. "And I didn't sign up to for this to be WCW. Bad enough I'm losing to James over there."

"You guys can do whatever you want," Spencer says, trying to sound just like the wrestlers' he's idolized throughout the years, confident and nonchalant. Like Tori's words didn't create a hole in his chest. "I'm out." He walks away from the living room and towards the door.

"Spence, wait," Tori says.

"Let him go," Billy says. "He's just throwing a hissy fit."

His hand on the door knob, Spencer stops. In his mind, he imagines Tori rushing over to him and forcing him to stop, tell him he's a vital part of RBWL. Or maybe stand with him and say that if he goes, so does she.

Neither of those two things happen, and the fantasies are left to be sucked into the hole in his chest, which grows bigger and bigger by the second. Spencer turns exits the apartment, before the hole sucks him in too.

CHAPTER SIX

SPENCER SPENDS THE FOLLOWING DAYS avoiding his brother and letting his eye heal. When Billy is in their bedroom, Spencer is in the living room watching television, the volume turned up as high as it can without waking up their dad. When Billy is in the living room, Spencer sequesters himself in their room and keeps the door shut, spending his time reading books he checks out of the library. When they are forced to share the same space, such as on the rare occasions the entire family gathers for a quick dinner, the numbers of words passed between brothers borders in the single digits, most ending up lying flat and useless on the kitchen table next to the micro- waved peas.

There is no talk of wrestling between them.

With Tori's help, Billy is able to line up several interviews. He's told their father about his job search, and with a promise to keep his grades up and put some of what he earns away for college, has his blessing. Often times, Spencer walks into the kitchen to find Billy and Tori hunched over the local want ads, Tori circling potential jobs and Billy grousing about how everything requires prior experience.

Whenever she sees Spencer, Tori smiles at him and tries to make small talk. She asks what good books he's read, if he's excited about sophomore year, and if he's watched this week's wrestling.

Spencer's answers are always short and to the point. Nothing she would like, not really, and no.

The knock on the apartment door comes on a Saturday, almost three weeks to the day since Spencer received his black eye. The sound pushes him out of a dream and forces his eyes open. Billy's bed is already made and empty.

The knocking continues.

"I'm up!" Spencer shouts. Untangling himself from his sheets, he puts on a pair of shorts and walks out of the bedroom. He notices the door to his father's room is closed and regrets yelling. The last thing their dad needs is to be woken up on his day off.

Scratching the back of his neck, Spencer tries to remember the dream he was having. Already the specific details of it are fading away, leaving him only with a twinge of excitement in the center of his chest. Whatever the dream had been about, it'd been a good one. Reaching the door, he swings it wide open and asks, "What?"

Tori stands in front of him, her fist frozen in mid knock. She's wearing a tight pair of blue jeans and a shirt which hangs loose off her shoulders. Spencer has never thought of himself as a clavicle man, but the subtle way Tori's clavicle creates two small, lovely mounds from which he can imagine his fingers traveling to on their way to her shoulders, makes him reconsiders what type of man he truly is.

"Billy's not here," Spencer says automatically.

"I know. Can I come in?"

Spencer nods and steps aside, allowing Tori to walk into the apartment. She heads straight for the kitchen table, Spencer noticing she's carrying a bulky gray laptop in one arm.

"What's your Wi-Fi password?" Tori asks, the laptop already open and her finger moving the blinking cursor across the dusty screen. "Never mind, one of your neighbor's keeps theirs unlocked."

Spencer closes the door behind him. "What's going on?"

Ignoring him, Tori directs the browser to a popular wrestling video sharing site, clicks on a link and turns the laptop in Spencer's direction. "Watch this."

The screen remains black long enough to make Spencer wonder if the laptop ran out of battery. Just when he's starting to get fidgety and sneak glances at Tori's naked shoulders, he hears music escaping out of its tiny speakers. Pixelated images flash across the laptop screen to the speeding rhythm of an electric guitar and the raw yells of a male singer. After a couple of seconds, the images start to slow down enough for Spencer to make them out.

"They do have a ring," he says and leans forward to get a better look.

To his annoyance, Spencer can only catch brief glimpses

of the structure, as whoever took the photos was more interested in highlighting The Woodland Terrace wrestlers than the ring. It's strange for Spencer to see how many of the photos resemble scenes straight out of Royal Brook's own shows. Some of the images show kids hitting each other with steel chairs and taking full on, unprotected headshots. Others feature guys his age and older replicating wrestling moves they've probably seen on television countless of times, with the photos capturing an awkwardness and clumsiness Spencer prays isn't featured in their own shows. There are also close ups of injuries, everything from long, bleeding gashes on foreheads, elbows and knees turned red and raw, and ugly black marks left on naked skin.

As the song comes to an end, so do the photos. The screen transitions to a shot of the back of an apartment building, a red cloth draped across the wall and the words WTF formed out of gray tape and placed on the center of it.

Eddie Tornado steps into the frame. Even through the dirty laptop screen, his mohawk is vibrant. Blue instead of the green he encountered, Spencer wonders if Eddie dips it in paint every night. The hair continues to lean to the left, as if weighted down by Eddie's ego. He stands bare-chested in the center of the frame, the black bruises on his ribs and chest like tumors against his pale skin. On his left shoulder rests a belt.

It's a Championship wrestling belt, with wide, black leather straps and five metal plates. The center plate is the largest by far, stretched into a thick, oval shape with two other square plates lining each of its sides. Eddie says nothing for the first minute and simply shines the center plate, running his hand over the lettering and ignoring the camera.

"How can they afford that?" Spencer asks, his left eye throbbing. "I checked online to see if we could have one made a while back, and those things cost hundreds of dollars."

Tori says nothing and turns up the volume on the laptop.

"Ladies and Gentlemen," Eddie begins, turning his attention to the camera. "Summer's almost over and man, where does the time fly? Feels like only yesterday when Insane Richie gave me this," he points to a not quite faded scar which starts on his right shoulder and runs down his bicep. "Of course, the bastard couldn't keep me from winning the WTF Championship." He stops and pats the belt.

"It's a pretty sight, ain't it?"

"Today's not about my accomplishments though. Today is all about our friends over at Royal Brooks. See, a couple of weeks ago one of their guys jumped me when I was at the movie theater. Fool just straight out tried to sucker punch me."

Spencer realizes Eddie's talking about him.

"I took care of him, like only Eddie Tornado can. But I guess I don't know my own strength. I kicked his ass so hard it put an end to their wrestling promotion. Haven't heard a peep from them in weeks. So, I figure I should apologize." Eddie puts his two hands together and continues, "Guys, I'm sorry y'all so pathetic you gave up so fast. I'm sorry you don't have a ring or even a real like belt like we do. And I'm especially sorry Tori has to be part of your sad little group."

Spencer glances at Tori. "He knows you?" Tori just stares at the screen.

"Everyone here knows Tor, right?" Eddie asks. The camera bobs up and down in response. "Yeah, I bet you guys do. I know her too. Real well. And it down right pains me to see her hanging around losers like Billy and Spencer Anderson. Thinking about her did give me an idea how I can make it up to RBWL though. I can give you all some nice memories to end the summer with." Reaching outside of the camera frame, Eddie comes back with a stack of Polaroid photos. He chooses one at random and motions to the camera to zoom in. When it does, its shows a grainy image of Tori on a bed. She isn't wearing anything. "Nice, huh? Yeah, I know you all like this. And I got tons more." Eddie plays with the stack, rearranging and running his thumb along the edges of the photos, like a card shark in a high-stake poker game. "Could show them to you all right now, but what would the fun be in that, right?"

Spencer isn't sure whether to be relieved or disappointed at this.

"Nah, what I think I'm going to do is wait until our next show. Get a projector in the middle of the ring and that way we can all have ourselves a little viewing party. Call it 'Tori's WTF debut'. Though I gotta tell you, I debuted three times this morning just looking through some of these pho—."

Tori closes the laptop.

Spencer is drowning in a sea of questions, rocked back and forth by everything he wants to ask Tori. When was this video posted? How do Eddie and Tori know each other? How did he get photos of her? *And does his brother know?*

"We used to go out," Tori says, as if reading his mind.

"He's an asshole."

Tori nods. "One of the many reasons I dumped him." A part of Spencer wants to look at the video again. And it isn't just to see how many photos Eddie shows of Tori. He wants to try to get a better look at their ring and wrestlers, dissect them and compare them against what they have here in RBWL. His fingertips itching, Spencer wishes he had a pen and his notebook.

"Spencer, hey, Spence? Did you hear what I asked?" Looking at Tori, Spencer admits he didn't.

She steps closer to him, close enough that he catches the scent of the lotion she uses. The coconut base infiltrates his nostrils and brings back the twinge of excitement he felt at waking up this morning. He almost misses her question again, but catches her lips moving and forces himself to focus.

"Will you help me get the photos back?"

CHAPTER SEVEN

SPENCER IS JERKED FORWARD as the bus comes to a stop. The doors open with a loud, pneumatic groan and a woman carrying an empty stroller steps inside, depositing her fare into the coin slot. He keeps his arms tightly folded across his chest and stares out the window, not wanting Tori to see the sweat stains forming around his armpits.

"You okay?" Tori asks.

Turning away from the window, Spencer gives Tori a smile. "Yeah, I'm good."

What about you? The words are held in bay. He wants to ask her how she's doing, but isn't sure he's equipped to handle the conversation.

"I just need you to be my lookout while I'm at Eddie's.

It'll be quick," she tells him.

"How are you getting in?" Spencer asks.

Tori reaches into her pocket and pulls out a set of keys. "Eddie gave them to me when we were dating."

"You guys must've been pretty serious."

"No, just stupid." Putting the keys back in her pocket, Tori leans back against the plastic seat and stares up to the ceiling of the bus. "Just so you know, when I knew him, he didn't go by Eddie Tornado. He didn't even have a mohawk. He was just a guy who I thought had a cute accent."

"Where did you meet him?"

Tori stays quiet for a moment and then answers. "We used to live in same building. Over in Woodland Terrace."

The admission makes Spencer's stomach drop faster than receiving a failing grade ever has. The logical part of his brain tells him there's no reason for him to feel betrayed. It wasn't like Tori could have guessed the rivalry which would end up forming between Royal Brooks and Woodland Terrace. He wonders if Billy knows.

"It was our first apartment after leaving Memphis," Tori continues. "We stayed there two years and then the rent went up, so we looked elsewhere."

"I didn't know you were from Memphis," Spencer says, wanting to put some distance between the thought of Tori and Eddie together.

"Why do you think I never eat what you Texans call 'barbecue'? We came here for daddy's work. Packed all our belongings in one single car and did the drive in a day."

Spencer packs away this new bit of information away, a rush of joy shooting across his temples at finding something new about Tori. "You miss Memphis?"

"All the time. Still think about my neighborhood. And the food. God I miss good, actual barbecue. You can sort of relate, huh? Billy's told me about how you guys had to move not too long ago."

"I guess," Spencer says.

"And the thing with your mom, that must have sucked." Spencer fidgets and makes a noncommittal sound. Reaching into his pocket, he takes out his black notebook and starts flipping through it.

The bus makes another stop and more people get in. When it starts moving again, Tori says, "Memphis is what got me into wrestling, you know."

Even though Spencer knows Tori is just using shorthand conversation to try to get him comfortable, it works. "Really?" he asks.

"Yeah, everyone there loves wrestling. I guess it's kinda like how Texas loves their football. Ingrained right into our blood or something. When did you get into it?"

"Billy never told you?"

"He's told me how *he* got into wrestling. But not you."

"Pretty much the same," Spencer says. He tells her about the nights watching wrestling with his family. How he and Billy both got so into it they would even watch the *lucha libre* shows which came on Sunday afternoon through the Spanish television station. How they graduated to watching the weekly Monday night shows and scouring the internet for the latest rumors of who was jumping promotion and what feuds where coming up next.

"I think I got into that more than anything else," he says.

"The whole behind the scenes thing is fascinating. How wrestlers will fight to keep their spots, who decides who wins the fake matches, things like that."

"It wasn't a big surprise to find out it was scripted?"

" "Not really. Part of me always knew, and whatever doubts I had were confirmed on the internet."

"I was shattered when I found out. Must have cried for days."

"Billy was the same way."

"And then we moved to Royal Brooks and I found out you guys were doing a backyard wrestling thing…"

"RBWL is not backyard wrestling," Spencer interrupts.

"Huh?"

Shifting in his seat, Spencer turns to look at Tori. "Backyard wrestling is pointless. It's just people wrestling with no rhyme or reason. The matches are all just about who can come out bloodier and doing something stupid. RBWL is not like that." Spencer taps his notebook. "Things are planned out. I make sure the matches have a pace and flow."

Tori raises her hands in surrender, "I didn't mean anything by it, Spencer, honest. I love what you do with RBWL. And I'm bummed that it's on pause."

Spencer takes a deep breath. "Sorry. Woodland Terrace is a backyard wrestling league. We're not."

"Speaking of which, our stop is coming up." Reaching across her seat, Tori pulls the cord above the window to signal the bus driver to stop. Spencer stays rigid both in posture and state, thrilled at the way Tori's body presses against his.

Woodland Terrace looks so much like Royal Brooks that

Spencer wonders if he could find his own doppelganger within the faded, beige, apartment buildings. The rental office sits a couple of yards away from them, the parking spaces labeled *Potential Renters* empty for the time being. As they cross the gates, Spencer expects alarm belts to starting ringing. The only sound he hears as they pass through is a thick, chewy bass line coming out of someone's nearby apartment.

Tori takes the lead. It isn't until they pass a small building lined with mailboxes that Spencer speaks up. "What if Eddie is there?"

"He won't be," Tori says, her eyes fixed straight ahead.

Spencer walks faster to catch up with Tori, the calves of his underworked legs stretching and screaming in frustration. "Are you sure? Shouldn't we come up with a plan, just in case?"

Tori turns and looks at Spencer. "They have a show today, okay?"

A bolt of surprise travels through Spencer, making his fingers tingle, rooting him to his spot. "I have to go see it," he says.

"There's no time. What if Eddie spots you?"

"I have to," Spencer says, knowing he sounds like a brat throwing a fit over a toy his mother won't let him have. But, he needs to see the wrestling show. A fear had settled in the back of his mind ever since he'd watched Eddie's video, a voice inside his head whispering how Woodland Terrace and Royal Brook's promotions both share the same amateurish look and wrestlers. Spencer is confident seeing the Woodland Terrace wrestlers live will silence that fear and show him the two promotions are nothing alike. That all Woodland Terrace has over Royal Brooks is a ring. All this is clearly laid out in his mind, but when he attempts to open his mouth and tell Tori, nothing comes out.

"I need your help today. You're the one I knew wouldn't freak out about the photos.," Tori says.

If Spencer focuses and turns his head at just the right angle, he's positive he can make out the sounds of the show. The hard slaps of the wrestlers meeting the ring mat, the cheers and boos of the crowd, and the tremor of the ring all tickle his ears and beckon him away from Tori.

But Tori's words cut through it all, becoming the mast he ties himself to.

"Let's go," he says. The words are out of his mouth before he can fully process his decision. The sounds of wrestling trickles away from him, and he wonders if they were just in his head to begin with. Smiling at him, Tori nods and resumes walking. Spencer falters a bit before following her. The realization there's very little he wouldn't do for Tori has sprung into his mind, and he's just smart enough to also realize how bad this could be.

CHAPTER EIGHT

HURRY UP, TORI, Spencer thinks, checking his watch for a third time. It's been ten minutes since she entered Eddie's apartment. Right before going in she handed Spencer a prepaid phone along with the number to an identical one she held in her hand. The plan was simple. Spencer was to text her if he saw anyone coming. So far, the only person Spencer had seen was an old man walking a little dog across the yard. Neither dog nor owner so much as glanced in Spencer's direction.

When Tori first told him to be her lookout, Spencer's mind flashed to his fantasy books and how they always contained a moment in which the hero would wait in the shadows, staying vigilant while sharpening his weapon. Upon arriving at Eddie's apartment however, Spencer found no shadows to hide under, and instead of the cool and collected lookout he thought he would be, Spencer is a speeding heart wrapped in a prickly bundle of tensed nerves. He spent the first few minutes pacing back and forth, until he realized doing so looked strange.

The door to one of the nearby apartments opens, Spencer thrusting his hands into his pocket and trying to look casual. He holds his breath until the woman who comes out closes the door behind her and walks away.

How hard can it be to find a couple of pictures anyways? he wonders.

Spencer's fingers touch the knot of fabric inside his pocket. Looking around to make sure he's still alone, Spencer pulls the fabric out and holds it with both hands.

The mask is bright blue with red and green accents around the set of eyeholes. Spencer runs his fingers across the stitching on the back and imagines what it must feel like to lace the mask up before a big match. He'd bought it in a garage sale, a slip of a character already jotted down in his notebook. But the mask arrived after Spencer and Billy had their big argument, and ended up being thrown in the back of the closet. He'd brought it with him figuring he could use it to hide his face, like he's seen people do on television when they're about to commit a crime.

This was before Tori told him his role.

He stuffs the mask back into his pocket and checks the time again. He looks out across the lawn, trying to figure out how far away the wrestling ring is, and whether he can head there and back without Tori noticing he's gone. He's just about made up his mind to give it try when he hears a loud crash coming from inside of Eddie's apartment.

"Tori?" He asks, staring at the door. "You okay?"

Spencer waits for a response, the cellphone out and his fingers on its keypad. He's almost lulled himself into believing he imagined the sound, when another crashing noise escapes out of the apartment.

"Stupid bitch!"

The words shatter Spencer's hesitation. He has the mask out and is opening the door to the apartment, with just enough time to slip the mask on before he's inside.

It sits lower on his face than expected, half his vision covered in the opaque fabric. The light around the apartment is distorted, with shadows jumping at him from every angle. The mask presses against his face and stifles his breathing. But he still feels better with it on. Almost like a different person.

And it's a good thing too, because fear squeezes his stomach. His eyes dart around the living room until he finds Tori. She's lying on the carpet, an overturned kitchen chair next to her. Standing over her is a large, bare chested guy, intricate knitted dreadlocks creeping down the back of his neck like thick bundles of ropes. Dreadlocks is clearly in better shape than Billy and a couple of inches taller than Carlos. Catching sight of him brings an itch to the back of Spencer's brain. He knows him from somewhere.

A yell vibrates in Spencer's throat, rising from an oily black pit he's dug deep within himself and used throughout childhood to dump all his anger and frustration. He catches-Dreadlocks off-guard, wrapping his arms around Dreadlock's neck and shifting his weight back in the hopes of bringing him down to the ground. There's a brief moment where the guy does take a step back, and Spencer is sure this is going to work. Then he regains his balance and with a quick flex of his hips sends Spencer flying. Spencer's head meets the sofa, the pain immediate and harsh. "Who the fuck are you?" Dreadlocks asks.

Spencer rubs the back of his head and says nothing. The shadows around his eyes are back, and he's not sure if the mask slipped further down or if he has a concussion.

He flinches when Dreadlocks kicks him in the leg.

"I asked you a question, asshole." One of Dreadlock's hand slams down on his shoulder, keeping him pinned against the ground. The other hand grabs the mask, getting a good chunk of Spencer's hair in the process. This is the moment Spencer's brain chooses to remember where he's seen Dreadlocks before. He's one of the wrestlers featured in the flyer Woodland Terrace passed around Royal Brooks. T.J. Payne, according to the name displayed below his image on the flyer.

"I don't know what the hell you two were planning to do here, but it ain't happening," Dreadlocks says.

Panic rises up as Spencer's mask starts to get pulled. He tries to fight and wiggle out of the man's grasp, but a kick to the ribs puts an end to that. Wheezing, Spencer's about to close his eyes and give up when he sees a shadow appear behind T.J.

Tori holds the kitchen chair in both hands. Spencer knows what's coming and just as he feels his mask pulled off. As the chair crashes down, Spencer expects the chair to break apart like he's seen happen in wrestling. The chair, however, stays in one piece, and a loud crack reverberating through the apartment, mingling with the surprised grunt T.J. gives just as he takes the full impact of the chair.

The hold on Spencer loosens and allows him to roll away just as T.J. pitches forward and crashes down on the sofa.

Both Tori and Spencer stare at T.J. The only sound in the apartment is Spencer's labored breaths. Setting the chair down, Tori steps over T.J, and offers Spencer her hand.

He takes it. "Thanks," he says.

Tori shakes her head. "I didn't know he would be here. I didn't think anyone would." She sits on the chair, running her hands through her hair. "Fuck, fuck, fuck. This was stupid."

"What happened?"

She looks up. "I was looking for the photos. When I was looking over there," she points to a shelf by the back of the room, "he suddenly comes up next to me. I think he must have been sleeping in Eddie's bedroom or something."

Spencer takes a second look at T.J. "You think he'll be okay?"

"Who cares." Tori stands. "We gotta go."

Spencer is about to agree when a thought stops him.

"Did you find the photos?"

"Forget about that. Let's just go before he wakes up."

Before Tori can stop him, Spencer runs towards the bedroom Tori said T.J. came out of. On his way he passes a closed door and wonders if there's someone waiting behind it ready to ambush them. This is almost enough to get him to listen to Tori, but Spencer has decided they've come too far now to go back empty handed. Besides, he's pretty sure anyone waiting would have come out by now.

Spencer steps inside Eddie's room. The place is a mess, with an unmade bed by the corner and a pizza box where a pillow should be. Spencer wades through an ocean of dirty laundry and glances at the posters taped to the walls. They alternate between bands he's never heard of and wrestlers he's very familiar with.

"What are you doing?" Tori stands in the doorway, arms folded across her chest. Every so often she checks back to the living room.

"Maybe the photos are here."

"You know how long it'll take us to go through this mess?"

Spotting a cluttered desk over by the corner Spencer moves to it and finds nothing there but old report cards and graded papers. To his surprise, Eddie is a decent student.

"Let's go, Spencer. We'll never find them in this mess," Tori says.

Spencer's about to give up when something in the bed catches his attention. Ignoring the crunch of stale chips under his feet, he makes his way to the bed and throws the covers on the floor.

He doesn't expect to see the tint of gold. The Woodland Terrace Championship belt hangs on the edge of Eddie's bed like a dog-eared copy of a favorite book would hang from his own bed. "Wow," he says, his hand feeling the smooth, cold leather of the straps.

"What?" Tori asks.

Grabbing the belt by the buckle, Spencer spins around and holds it high in the air. The belt has a wonderful, real weight to it, and Spencer wants nothing more than to put it around his own waist. The only thing holding him back is the fear that the straps, long as they are, won't be long enough to go around his waist.

"What is that doing here?" Tori asks, stepping into the room.

"I don't know. Didn't you tell me they were putting on a show today?"

"They were. I mean, they are."

"We're taking it," Spencer says, the words out of his mouth as soon as he thinks them. "We can hold it ransom and trade it back for the photos."

"You're crazy…"

Spencer throws the belt back on the bed and starts looking around the room. "It'll work, I promise. It's what would have happen during the Monday Night Wars."

"The what? And what are you looking for now?"

"Something to put the belt in, just in case we come across anyone on our way out." Spencer is about to explain to Tori all about the golden age of wrestling—the time period in the late nineties in which the two national wrestling promotions fought for ratings and market shares when she speaks up again.

"We need to go, Spencer. *Now.*"

"Just a second. There has to be something here we can use. There," he points to the closet door, propped open by a blue gym bag. Grabbing the belt off the bed, he moves to the closet and picks up the gym bag. It's heavier than he expected, and if Spencer goes by Terri's room, he guesses there's a couple of months' worth of dirty workout clothes inside. He crams the belt in without looking and zips up the bag.

"Ready," he says, putting the bag's strap over his shoulder. Tori stays in her spot, looking at him with a strange, lopsided smile. "What?" Spencer asks.

"You just reminded me of your brother."

He's not quite sure whether to take that as a compliment or not. Readjusting the bag, he follows Tori out of Eddie's room.

"Hey," he says as they pass the closed door in the hallway, "maybe we should check in there."

"I don't want to risk it. Besides, that's his dad's room, and trust me, nothing of Eddie's would be there."

Spencer eyes the door, wanting to know what she means by that. But before he can ask her, they come to the living room. To his immediate relief, T.J. is still sprawled on the sofa exactly where they left him. Another thing where real life was different from wresting—in the television shows the wrestlers always got up after a few minutes, regardless of how many chair shots they took. Closing the door to the apartment behind them, they head to the exit of the apartment complex without speaking. Spencer keeps a tight hold on the strap of the bag and constantly checks behind them. No one stops them.

They're lucky in that they don't have to wait long for a bus. It's not until they're a couple of blocks away from Woodland Terrace that Spencer lets out the breath he's been holding. They sit at the far end of the bus, Tori's eyes closed and her head down. Spencer is next to her, the bag on his lap. He opens it.

"Uh, Tori?" he says, staring at the contents of the gym bag, "You need to look at this."

Opening one eye, Tori says, "Can it wait, till we get to Royal Brooks, Spencer? I have a big headache."

"I think you better look at it."

Tori groans and lifts her head up to look at the bag. Spencer makes sure to tilt it in her direction so she can see exactly what he did.

"Holy fuck," she says.

"I know." Spencer drops the bag back on his lap and stares down at it. The belt is there, and continues to be an impressive sight, but it's what's under the belt that made Spencer call out to Tori. There are no dirty workout clothes in the gym bag, only what looks like hundreds of individually and tightly wrapped baggies. The belt is floating on a sea of green haze and the smell that's released instantly makes Spencer dizzy.

Marijuana. A bag full of it.

"I guess we know how they can afford the ring," Tori says.

CHAPTER NINE

SPENCER STANDS IN THE DOORWAY of their apartment. The door is shut behind him and the living room lights are turned off. The silence coils around him, the darkness of the room allowing Spencer to imagine he stepped outside the real world and into his own small, private pocket of nothingness. It isn't long however before reality intrudes in the form of a tingling sensation on his right arm. Spencer tries to ignore it for as long as he can, but the tingling yanks him back to his apartment and to the heavy gym bag he holds in his hand.

The sound the bag makes when it hits the floor causes Spencer to wince and closes the pocket once and for all.

Rubbing his arm, Spencer turns the living room light on. He does the same for the kitchen, the bulbs flickering in and out, as if they are having trouble remembering how to function. Adjusting to the fluorescent lights, Spencer looks around the cluttered kitchen. He's only been away a couple of hours, but the apartment seems different somehow, as if everything has been moved a couple of inches to the left.

At least he's alone.

A grumbling stomach sends Spencer to the refrigerator. He has the bread, ham, and cheese out and on the kitchen counter before he notices the note. It's stuck to the refrigerator thanks to a googly-eyed clam magnet someone on vacation once sent them. The note is from their dad, the blue handwriting slant and light on the notepad. He's working late, it says, but he's leaving Spencer and Billy twenty dollars to get something to eat. The note ends with a directive for the two of them to behave.

Spencer checks and sure enough, there are two ten dollar bills behind the note. After the day he's had, Spencer is happy to have the place all to himself.

He spent most of the bus ride too nervous to relax, the gym bag resting on his lap. Tori didn't say much on the way home, with Spencer figuring she was busy replaying the day's events much like he was. When the bus dropped them off at Royal Brooks, Tori told him she had a headache and it was best if they both just talked later. Spencer didn't even get a chance to ask her what he should do with the gym bag before she walked away.

Spencer stares at the bag. Alone with it, a question he's been pushing out of his mind ever since they left Eddie's apartment rises to the surface.

Now what?

It's a question which pulsates in the center of Spencer's

brain and stretches his head. All Spencer wants to do is forget about the bag and walk away.

But he can't. Not entirely. With a sigh, he picks the bag once more and carries it to his bedroom. The individual hairs of the carpet seem to come alive as he walks, latching on to his feet and making each of his steps a struggle. His fingers ache and he shifts the bag to his other hand, tempted to just call it quits and lie on the hallway itself.

It's the crash that comes after a bunch of adrenaline is dumped into your body. He's trying to recall whether that's an actual thing that happens or if he just read about it in one of his books when Spencer steps into his room and catches sight of his unmade bed. The pillow propped up against the wall and the set of rumpled blankets invite him to return back to the pocket of nothingness from before.

Dropping the bag on the floor, he has just enough energy left to push it under his bed and then kick his shoes off. By the time Spencer's head lands on the pillow, he's already given in fully to sleep.

Eddie's laughter infiltrates his sleep like a worm burrowing into the soft earth. Spencer's eyes snap open, clarity floating just out of his reach. His mouth is dry, with the headache still occupying the same space in his head. Spencer's entire body is sore and begging him not to move. He wonders if this is what being hungover feels like.

Spencer almost fools himself into thinking he dreamed up Eddie's laughter when he hears it again. Untangling himself from the blankets, Spencer rolls out of bed. The glowing digital face of the nearby clock tells him he slept for almost three hours. Reaching down to the floor, Spencer picks up a stray barbell from Billy's side of the room.

He found out about the bag, Spencer thinks. His eyes lock into the bottom of his bed, where somewhere among old comics, overdue library books, and fast food wrappers, Eddie's weed and Championship belt lie. Holding the barbell up in the same position he's watched ninjas hold their swords in countless of late night cable movies, Spencer edges out of the room and into the hallway. The smooth, cold metal is a stranger in his hands, but it helps to reassure him. Gripping the bar tightly, he stretches his ear out towards the living room and listens.

Nothing.

A glow ekes out of the room, painting one end of the hallway in yellow. He stops at the edge of the hall, where the carpet takes on the glow of the living room, presses against the wall, and waits. Waits and imagines Eddie somewhere in the apartment. Maybe he's sprawled on their couch watching their television. Or foraging through their kitchen, peeking inside their refrigerator and kitchen cabinets. Perhaps the laughter Spencer heard is Eddie discovering the bargain brand cereal they buy, the one which comes in large clear bags and grows stale after a week, no matter how hard they tie the ends together.

"You can come out, Spencer."

The voice belongs to his brother, and it surprises Spencer to the point he almost drops the barbell. He doesn't immediately do as Billy says, instead flashing back to the moment when the laughter woke him. He didn't image Eddie's laugh,

Spencer's sure of that. Which means Eddie could still be in the living room somewhere, maybe holding Billy hostage. It's either that or… *Shit.*

Spencer pivots out of the hallway and into the living room, barbell in hand. He finds his brother sitting at the kitchen table, Tori's laptop in front of him.

"Hey, Billy, when did you get home?" Spencer asks. Realizing he's still holding the barbell, he sets it down on the floor.

"A while ago," Billy says, his eyes never leaving the computer screen. There is no sign of Eddie anywhere.

"I don't know if you saw Dad's note. He left us some money. If you feel like ordering pizza, I think we have enough for that and some wings. Or maybe you want to walk over to Taco Cabana and get something there?"

"You seen Tori?"

Gulping down the rest of his food suggestions, Spencer stares at his brother.

"I mean, this is her computer," Billy says, tapping the top of the laptop. "Right?

Spencer nods. "She stopped by earlier."

Grunting, Billy turns back to the laptop screen.

"What you looking at?"

Billy looks up and without a word turns the computer around. While expected, Spencer's stomach rolls and tumbles down a dark pit when he sees Eddie frozen on the computer screen, his mouth a cavernous opening from which trouble will spew the moment Billy clicks play again.

"You see this?" Billy says.

The room is tilting to a nauseating degree. "Tori showed it to me," Spencer says.

"God damn it, she's not answering her phone now. Did you see everything in this fucking video? The photos too?"

Spencer hesitates, and Billy notices. Closing the laptop, Billy pulls back his chair and tells Spencer, "I'm going to kill him. The words hang between them, their edges sharp with a simplicity Spencer knows to be true.

"Fuck up Eddie's whole damn world for this," Billy says.

"I'm sorry," Spencer says, stepping in front of his brother and raising his arms to stop him. "Let me explain first."

"You don't have explain nothing, Spence. You're not the asshole in this, Eddie is. After I'm done with him, we can talk. Get back to putting on RBWL shows like we should have been doing this whole time." Billy gently pushes past Spencer and heads to their room. Spencer follows.

"What are you going to do?" he asks his brother, who is rooting through their closet.

"I already told you, kill him."

Spencer glances to his bed for a second. "Don't be stupid." he says.

Billy comes out of the closet with a pair of black boots. Sitting on the edge of his bed, he starts to lace them up. "Stupid is letting this thing go on for as long as it has. Stupid is fighting against each other, when we really should have been focusing on Eddie and Woodland Terrace. Shit, the more I think about it, this is probably the smartest thing I've done in a while." He grins at Spencer.

Spencer stares at his brother, trying to figure out if he's

serious about going out and committing murder. He wants to think Billy isn't that foolish, but all it takes is one good look at the way he's cloaked in bravado and determination to know his brother is about to do something stupid.

Billy has his boots laced up when Spencer understands the only thing which will keep Billy in this room. The thing fits so neatly into the day's events that it makes Spencer dizzy all over again.

"Wait, Billy," he says, kneeling down and reaching underneath his bed. "There's something I need to show you."

CHAPTER TEN

"THIS IS INSANE," Spencer hisses.

"Calm down," his brother says and takes another bite of his taco. A rain of tomatoes, onions, and meat escape out of the tortilla and land on the plate below. Billy points to the solitary taco left on a red tray and asks, "Either of you guys going to eat that?"

Two days have passed since Spencer pulled Eddie's gym bag from under his bed and showed it to Billy. His brother's original disbelief was silenced when Spencer opened the bag and held the Championship belt out. Billy only had one question after that;

'Why didn't she ask for my help?'

Spencer couldn't give him an answer, so Billy went out to get it from Tori herself, with Spencer not far behind. Spencer got as far as Tori's apartment before Billy slammed the door shut in his face. Whatever Billy and Tori discussed inside her apartment is unknown to Spencer, as he got stuck waiting outside for over an hour before being let in. All three now sit around a table inside a local taqueria.

The smoke from the grill escapes out of the nearby kitchen and lace the air with spices. Music from a jukebox sitting by the corner pumps out an '80s' rock song. It's noon, and the place is packed with a mix of families and people on their lunch break.

Spencer pushes the tray in his brother's direction. "This is insane," he repeats, turning to look at Tori for help.

"Maybe he has a point, Billy," she says, reaching over and picking some of the stray barbacoa meat off the plate.

"Why, because I thought of it instead of you?" Billy bites down on the taco. "After what you two did, calling anything insane is a dumb."

Tori shakes her head. "You going to be an asshole to me much longer?"

Using a piece of tortilla to sop up the remaining salsa, Billy says, "I'm not an asshole."

"You've been pissy since you found out about the bag. And I get it, Billy, I do. I should have told you what I was planning to do…"

"You should have told me everything," Billy interrupts. "*Everything.*"

"Billy," Tori says, not unkindly, "I'm sorry about not telling you about the video. But screw you if you think I'm going to apologize for who I dated before you. And if you don't stop acting like a total asshole, I'll leave."

Billy and Tori stare at each other from across the plastic table. A Spanish song plays from the jukebox. Spencer waits to see who in the table will blink first.

Turns out it's Billy, who picks up the red tray and walks to the trash can with it. Tori watches him go and flicks a piece of onion off the table. "Your brother can be a real douchebag," she tells Spencer.

"Didn't you use to call him charming?" Spencer asks.

Tori laughs and punches Spencer on the shoulder. "If I had to choose, I'd pick you as the charmer of the two."

Her words bring a fire to Spencer's cheeks and a tickling down his spine. He takes a drink of his horchata, too afraid to open his mouth and have something the opposite of charming escape out.

Billy returns, throwing himself back into his chair. He folds his arms across his chest and says to Tori, "You should have come to me first."

"We've been over this. I thought you would react poorly. I have no idea why I thought that," Tori says with a motion of her hand.

"This isn't funny," Billy says. "I'm your boyfriend."

"Are you? Cause you haven't acted like one for the last few days."

"Those photos—"

"Are my past," Tori cuts Billy off. "And you don't get to judge me because of it. Not if you still want to be my boyfriend."

"I'm just saying, you could have at least—"

"Stop."

Tori's words force Billy to chew down whatever he was

going to say to her. Spencer watches with fascination, having never seen his brother withdraw from an argument.

"Fine. I'm just saying, it sucked that you went to Spencer first." He turns to Spencer and says, "No offense."

Before Spencer can take offense, a hand slams down on his back and a voice asks, "No offense to what?"

"Nothing," Spencer says, arching his back to lessen the sting of the slap.

Carlos pulls out the chair next to Spencer and sits down. He glances around the table and takes a bite out of the churro he's holding in his hand.

"About time you got here," Billy says.

"I said sixish." Carlos wipes his hands on his jeans and asks, "And why are you all here? I thought it was just going to be you, Billy."

"It's all three of us or no one," Spencer says. "That's the deal."

"What deal? What are guys talking about?" Carlos looks around the table and frowns. "I feel like I'm missing something."

Tori, Billy, and Spencer came up with the deal while sitting on the floor of Tori's bedroom, Eddie's bag in the center of their makeshift circle and the Woodland Terrace belt slathered atop it like the extra toppings on an overloaded slice of pizza. All three agreed whatever happened next with the bag, they would all be involved. No more keeping anyone in the dark.

"Never mind," Billy tells Carlos. "We ready to go?"

Carlos checks his watch. "They should be letting people in now. You brought the stuff, right?"

Billy nods and reaches down to his feet, where Spencer knows Eddie's bag has been the whole time. "Your guy will be there?"

"Dude," Carlos says, "don't make it sound gay. But yeah, he'll be there."

"And he's willing to buy this off us?"

"Long as what you got is legit."

"Cool," Billy says and stands. He places the bag on his chair while he takes out his wallet and dumps a couple of dollar bills on the table.

Spencer tenses at the appearance of the gym bag. He looks around the restaurant and its tightly packed tables, positive one of them is occupied by a stable of undercover cops waiting to and snap handcuffs on them all. But if there are cops around, they're all too invested in the plates of food in front of them to pay any attention to four teenagers and a gym bag.

"Come on, Spencer, let's go." Tori prods him on his side, and when Spencer looks up, Carlos and Billy are already walking to the front of the restaurant.

"You think Billy is going to stop being an asshole?" Spencer asks as they exit the restaurant.

"I hope so. You really think this idea is that insane?"

"I'd feel better if it didn't rely on Carlos," Spencer says. They join the crowd walking over to the crossing intersection. Spencer spots Carlos and Billy already on the other side of the street, in front of a large, brick building.

"All he has to do is introduce us. Even Carlos can't screw

that up," Tori says. "Besides we need him. It's not like we know anyone else who'll buy Eddie's stuff."

"What took you guys so long?" Carlos asks Spencer and Tori when they reach the other side.

"Would've been nice if you two waited for us," Spencer says. He points to the line forming by the doors of the building. "Shouldn't we be over there?"

"You guys gotta relax, man. This is going to be fun times," Carlos says, handing each of them a ticket. "By the way, you guys owe me twenty bucks for the tickets. And, you know, my cut."

The four of them walk towards the back of the line, Spencer lagging behind as he looks down at the ticket Carlos gave him. It's a small, brown stub with a black number eight printed on both sides. It gives no hint as to what it grants them access to.

The large banner hung above the building's doors on the other hand does. In red letters it reads:

EXTREME TEXAS PRO WRESTLING ONE NIGHT ONLY!

CHAPTER ELEVEN

SPENCER'S TICKET IS RIPPED in half by a disinterested looking girl sitting behind a table. Without looking up from the magazine she's reading, the girl points to the arrows taped to the wall. The directions aren't needed, as all Spencer has to do is head towards the set of blue doors at the end of the hallway, where the hum of a crowd escapes out every time they're opened.

The white walls of the Dallas community center are plastered with motivational posters imploring passersby to take SAT prep classes, sign up for a weekly bowling league, and let people know about an upcoming neighborhood yard sale. Spencer passes a poster featuring a teen with coifed hair, and it takes him a second to recognize him as the star of a television show which went off the air a couple of years ago. In the poster, the teen is telling kids drugs are for losers, ironic considering Spencer is pretty sure the teenager is now in rehab.

When they reach the end of the hall, they find another person checking for tickets.

"You guys ever been here before?" Carlos asks, lining up behind a large guy with a shaved head and stretched out ears holes.

Spencer shakes his head and Billy says, "We kept meaning to. Never seemed to have the cash."

"They put on a good show. Don't expect pay-per-view quality matches or nothing, but they're fun. Sometimes they even snag a couple of the castoffs from the big boys."

Spencer wants to ask Carlos for examples of the wrestlers Extreme Texas Pro Wrestling has managed to get, but before he knows it he's in the front of the line. "Enjoy the show," the guy says after running a black marker across Spencer's ticket. The wrestling mask he wears muffles his words. The mask is so similar to the one Spencer wore when robbing Eddie he can't help but stare at it until Billy shoves him forward and says, "Hurry up."

Spencer walks through the blue doors and into the community center's gymnasium, repurposed into a wrestling arena for today's activities. The back wall is lined with tables loaded with shirts, posters, and other merchandise for fans to buy. Some of the wrestlers stand behind their tables, looking just as bored as the girl who took Spencer's ticket, but others mingle in front of the small crowd, posing for photographs and signing autographs.

The rest of the gym is filled with rows of folding chairs, about half of them currently taken up by wrestling fans. The crowd is mostly male, around Spencer's age, and clad in shirts referencing either wrestling or comic books. Spencer also spots a couple of adults in the crowd, some who are clearly fans of the product and others who judging from their perplexed look on their faces, have been dragged here by their children. All the chairs surround the wrestling ring sitting in the center of the court.

Spencer steps forward. He doesn't pay attention to the match taking place in the ring, his attention on the structure itself. It looks regulation size, just like the one Spencer has seen every Monday night on television. How the ropes react when one of the wrestlers is thrown against them, they could do with being a bit looser. He wouldn't have the ropes be that shade of red, but otherwise they seem legit. There's even a set of steel steps over by the corner. Well, maybe not steel, but they *look* steel, which is the important part.

"You okay, Spencer?" Tori moves and stands next to him. "You sort of zoned out back there," she says, motioning to the doors.

"Yea, I'm okay," Spencer says.

Tori squeezes his shoulder. "Soon you'll have enough money to get RBWL its own very ring."

"What are you guys talking about?" Billy asks, squeezing in between Spencer and Tori.

"Your plan," Spencer says.

"And how genius it is?"

"Something like that. Hey, shouldn't we be following Carlos?" Tori asks, pointing at the Mexican who is already heading to the back of the gym.

"Come on," Billy says, "we'll have plenty of time to see the rest of the show afterwards."

Taking one last look at the ring, Spencer follows his brother and Tori as they catch up with Carlos. People continue to stream into the gym, filling the seats around them. Every so often, the crowd lets out a big cheer. The sound crests from one side of the room to the other, sending a shiver down Spencer's spine. The cheers also wash away some of the tension knotted deep between his shoulder blades. As loud as the cheers are, Spencer can't help but think about how it's just a fraction of cheers that big promotions—the ones with television and pay-per-view deals—get in a nightly basis.

And it's still louder than anything he'll ever be able to produce in RBWL, ring or no ring.

The thought should be demoralizing. But Spencer finds much like when he was told all he had to do to pass his P.E class was finish one lap around the football field compared to everyone else's three. There's a certain comfort to knowing you're in no danger of ever overachieving.

Carlos waits for them by the last row of seats, just a couple of feet away from the entrance stage. It's built entirely out of a combination of cardboard, duct tape, and Christmas lights. There's no ramp, just a path to the ring created by separating the rows of chairs straight down the middle. They reach Carlos just in time to see a bearded wrestler come through the red curtain hanging from the stage. A fog machine kicks in and *One* by Metallica blares out speakers lined against the sides of the gym. The crowd halfheartedly boos the wrestler as he walks to the ring. Carlos waits for the wrestler to be close to the ring before heading in the direction of the entrance stage. Spencer, Tori, and Billy follow him, with Spencer assuming they're going through the curtains. Instead, Carlos skips the stage altogether and walks to the far end of the gym, where there is set of doors Spencer hadn't noticed before.

These are the doors the wrestlers are actually walking through, Spencer realizes. While the crowd focuses on the action happening in the ring, the wrestlers slip in and wait behind the entrance stage until it's their cue to come out. It's yet another example of the sleight of hand so ingrained into the wrestling business.

You guys ready?" Carlos asks, his hand on the door. "No going backsies at this point, you know."

"Can we just get this thing over with?" Spencer asks.

"Yeah, yeah, I just want to make sure we're on the same page here. Don't want this thing to go down the shitter and me not getting a cut. And trust me, if you guys are as on edge as you are right now, Mike is going to think something's up and call the whole thing off. Took me forever to even convince him to meet us." Checking to make sure the crowd has their attention on the ring, Carlos pulls the door open.

"How do you even know him?" Billy asks when they're all on the other side of the door.

"He dated my mom for a while."

Carlos' words echo in the hall as they walk. The hallway has the same sort of smell Spencer learned to dread during school hours. It's a combination of sweat, the insides of tennis shoes, and dirty laundry, all combining to create something that will stick to their clothing for the next day or so.

"He's a cool dude, if a little bit odd sometimes."

Spencer and Tori share a look. Like Spencer, she's probably wondering how strange a person has to be in order for Carlos to consider them odd.

"I think he was a truck driver at the time. Or maybe he was still selling makeup door to door. He's always been the guy with the hook up though. Looked him up not too long ago and found he was doing this now."

"Guy has had a lot of jobs," Tori says.

"What can I say, dude's a modern renaissance man."

Spencer doesn't have time to be in awe over Carlos using the word 'renaissance' correctly, the hallway veering to the left and leading them directly into the men's locker room, currently occupied by a dozen or so different wrestlers. Some of them are changing in and out of their gear, consisting of everything from standard wrestling trunks, to a guy off in the corner struggling with a full bunny outfit. *He probably should have put the head on last*, Spencer thinks. Others sit off by themselves or in groups of two and threes, quietly talking to each other as they ice knees and shoulders. Spencer desperately wants to know what they're talking about. He wants to go to them and compare notes, see how planning out a match for twenty people differs from planning a match for a couple of hundred people.

Billy, Carlos, and Tori step into the locker room without missing a beat, but Spencer hesitates at the threshold. He hasn't earned being in a place like this, not when he can't even keep a simple backyard promotion going. *Maybe that's why Carlos didn't want me here,* Spencer thinks. He's almost talked himself into walking away when he hears his name being called.

It's Billy, motioning to Spencer with his free hand while grinning the whole time. Seeing his brother and the stupid, confident grin splayed out across his face is infectious, and prompts Spencer to step into the room. He expects every wrestler to immediately turn his way and sniff him out as a pretender, but his entrance is ignored by everyone but Billy, who grins even wider and walks up to him.

"These guys aren't anything special, Spence. Shit, I'm in better shape than half of them," he says, putting his arm around Spencer's shoulder.

Together they follow Carlos.

CHAPTER TWELVE

ARM STILL AROUND HIM, Billy leads Spencer to the far end of the locker room, where Carlos and Tori stand next to a balding man putting a black and white striped shirt on. "So after your mama and me split, I headed to Vegas. Figured I'd do a stint out as a cabbie, earn some quick bucks, and see some shit." The man says, looking up when Billy and Spencer reach him. "This the guy?" he asks, pointing to Billy.

"Yea, that's the guy," Carlos says.

"Stuff's inside I take it," Mike says, looking at the bag Billy's been carrying.

Nodding, Billy steps forward and begins to open the bag.

"What the fuck, dude? Don't start pulling shit out here," Mike says. Shaking his head, he looks to Carlos and tells him, "Christ, maybe this was a mistake."

"Wait, what?" Spencer says. "No."

Mike tilts his head and looks at Spencer. "And you are?"

"He's no one," Carlos tells Mike.

"Screw you, Carlos. I'm the one who—"

"Spencer!" Tori says.

"Shut up," Billy hisses.

Mike pays no attention to either of them and keeps his eyes on Spencer. "What happened, you find it at the bottom of your hundredth happy meal?"

"No I—"

Billy elbows Spencer before he can finish his sentence. "You want it or not, man?" he asks Mike.

Mike leans back on his chair and scratches his belly. "Maybe."

"Come on Mike," Carlos says, "you're making me look bad here."

"And how you think I look right now, talking to a bunch of fuckheads whose balls haven't dropped yet?" Mike says, turning to Tori. "You're probably the smartest of them all, just 'cause you haven't said a word."

"So do business with me then," Tori says.

Mike laughs. "Cute. And what do you know about business, girlie?"

"I know we're offering you a good deal," Tori says. "We're not even asking for half what it's worth."

"Why?" Mike asks.

"Why what?" Tori asks.

Shaking his head, Mike reaches down to tie his sneakers. "Come on, business-girl, keep up. Why?"

Billy, Spencer, and Tori all glance at each other, and it is

Carlos who finally speaks up. "He wants to know why you guys are willing to let it go for so low if the stuff's worth so much. God, guys, you're really embarrassing me here."

Mike snaps his fingers and says, "Bingo." Standing up, he stretches out his arms and legs, before rolling his shoulders. "Listen, I gotta go out and be the ref for this lumberjack match, so why don't you all stick around try to figure out a reason as to why I should do *business* with you all." Stretching his legs one final tie, Mike joins the rest of the wrestlers who are heading out the door. A couple of the wrestlers glance back to look at Spencer and the rest of the group, but if they question why four kids are staying behind in the locker room, they don't do it aloud.

Spencer assumes they're the only ones left in the room, but a quick check reveals the person in the bunny costume still in the corner. Having not gotten much further than putting on the head, he or she now lays on one of the locker room benches, asleep. Or dead.

"So, what do we tell Mike when he comes back?" Billy asks, dropping the bag on the floor.

"That we found it?" Spencer says.

"What did you tell him in the first place, Carlos?" Tori asks. "Wasn't he curious about you coming to him with an offer to sell him a bag full of weed out of nowhere?"

"Nah. He just told me to drop by here."

Spencer frowns. "So why does he care now?"

"I dunno, maybe he's had some time to think about it. What do I look like, a mind reader?"

"You guys don't find that a bit weird?" Spencer asks. "He

brings us out here, and all of sudden he doesn't want to buy the bag?"

Carlos looks at Spencer. "Dude, didn't you hear me before? Mike's weird."

"No one's saying he doesn't want to buy the bag," Billy adds. "Guy's just playing hardball."

Spencer looks at the bag and then to his brother and Tori. "This was a mistake."

"Spencer, calm down, man," Billy says.

"You heard Carlos. Mike didn't even question him about the bag. Who does that?"

"If you bail now, no way am I lining up another meeting," Carlos says.

Billy ignores Carlos. "Spencer, maybe you should go out and watch the show. We can handle things here."

"We should go. I don't like this," Spencer says, glancing to Tori for help.

Tori won't meet his eyes. "We're already here, Spence. And yeah, the guy's a little bit weird, but so what? I think your brother's right."

The bridge of Spencer's nose pulsates with the birth of a headache. He takes a step back, Tori's words still circling around his ears. Spencer glances at the gym bag on the floor and nods.

"Fine," he says.

"It's for the best," Billy says. "That way we do the heavy lifting and you—"

Spencer lunges for the bag, wrapping his hands around its handles and pushing forward with the heels of his feet. He's heading to the locker room exit before the other three can react.

"What the fuck are you doing!" Spencer hears his brother shout. Gripping the bag even tighter, Spencer keeps his eyes locked on the exit. The center of his chest burns and his lungs feel like they're about to explode, but he's almost there. He tries not to think about the stretch of hallway awaiting him, focusing only on the idea of getting out of the locker room with the bag. He hears footsteps behind him.

The exit is only one or two steps away when a shadow fills the doorway. Spencer has just a second to notice it before Dreadlocks appears.

Time doesn't slow down. If anything, it moves faster. One moment Spencer is trying to pivot and turn away from the exit and the next Dreadlocks has him by the collar. Spencer manages to catch a glimmer of Billy's confused, shocked face and hear Tori let out a yell of surprise before Dreadlocks has one hand on his neck and the other on his arm. "Remember me, asshole?" he asks Spencer.

"Spencer!" Tori shouts.

"Let go of him," Billy adds in unison as he, Carlos, and Tori all come to a stop.

Spencer tries to wiggle out of Dreadlocks grasp, prompting the large man to tighten his hold. "Shut the fuck up," Dreadlocks tells the three of them before shaking Spencer, "And you better stop moving, or I'll swear I'll snap your neck."

"I'd do what he asks," a voice comes from the back of the locker room. "T.J. is still kind hurting over the way you guys left him."

Like something out of a nightmare, the man with the bunny head rises from his bench like the Frankenstein monster rising from his slab. Even before he takes off the head, Spencer knows who it is.

"Shit, you have no idea how hot it gets inside that thing." He's soaking in sweat, his mohawk bleeding down all his face. He kicks the bunny head and it goes sailing across the opposite side of the locker room. Pushing his hair away from his face, Eddie grins and says, "What's up doc?"

CHAPTER THIRTEEN

A 'TOLD YOU SO' bubbles behinds Spencer's lips, and it takes all his willpower to squash it down.

"What a god damn amazing swerve this is, right?" Eddie asks, striding towards Billy, Carlos, and Spencer. "I ain't gonna lie, it was hard to stay on that bench there while you assholes tried to get rich off my hard work, but damn if it wasn't worth it to see y'all faces when the hammer dropped." He stands in front of Carlos, Tori, and Spencer and shouts, "BOOM," laughing when the three of them flinch.

"Just take your bag," Billy says through clenched teeth.

"Oh shit, may I? You hear that, T.J.?" Eddie says and steps closer to Billy. "This asshole here is giving me permission to take back the bag his fat ass of a brother stole from us. Ain't he polite?"

At the mention of the theft, T.J. presses harder on Spencer's neck. Eddie takes a step and with a quick motion punches Billy in the stomach. Billy lets out a grunt and falls to his knees. Eddie steps on Billy's hand with his left foot and knees him on the ribs.

"Who the hell y'all think you are, giving me permission to take back my own property? You damn right I'm taking the bag. MY bag. What each of you should be doing is kissing my ass and hoping I don't beat the shit out." He turns around and looks at each of them one by one before walking closer to Billy and Tori.

"Stop it!" Tori says, pushing Eddie away. She kneels next to Billy and checks on him.

Eddie looks down at Tori. "Should've dumped you sooner, you back stabbing bitch."

"I dumped you. Or did you forget all the whiny messages you left afterwards?" Tori says, helping Billy back to his feet. "You got your bag back now, just leave."

"Shit, were you this stupid when I was going out with you?" Eddie asks Tori before pointing to Spencer. "In fact, bring that fat-ass over here," he orders T.J. "He needs to share in the punishment as well."

Spencer's heart quickens when T.J. lets go of his neck and pushes him forward to join the rest of the group. Eddie stands with arms folded, clearly enjoying his moment.

"Y'all really thought you could get away with this, huh? Didn't you think that maybe, just maybe, Mike, would come to the one guy he knows deals around this parts ask if he's heard about a new group trying to make move in?"

When Eddie puts it like that, it does sound foolish. Once

again the words 'I told you so,' threaten to spill out of Spencer's mouth.

"Mike wouldn't do that, he's my friend," Carlos says.

"No, buddy," Eddie says, his words dripping with so much saccharine Spencer almost expects to find a puddle on the ground. "He's your dealer. Or would be if you had any money."

"Fuck you, Carlos says.

"It's the truth, man. Looks like you're going to have to find a new daddy."

Carlos vibrates, his hands closing into fists. Spencer catches the look which passes between Carlos and Billy, seconds before they both rush Eddie.

Spencer knows it's a mistake.

He knows it because T.J. never moves from his spot. He knows it because Eddie yawns and reaches for the waistband of his shirt, pulling out a gun and pointing it with a frustrating casualness at Carlos and Billy.

The harsh light of the locker room bounces off the weapon's slick matte finish. The muzzle is a tiny, dark opening, so small Spencer has a hard time understanding how it could cause harm to anyone.

"Told you I was going to have to bust this out," he tells T.J. Walking over to Carlos. Eddie leans forward until his nose is almost touching the Mexican's. "Not so brave now, huh?" Before Carlos can answer, Eddie slaps him hard across the face with the gun. Carlos topples over.

"Get me the stuff," Eddie tells T.J.

Grabbing the bag out of Spencer's hand, TJ walks over to Eddie and unzips it.

Glancing inside it, Eddie frowns. "What the hell is that?" In between two of his fingers T.J. holds a pair of Odor-Eaters.

"To hide the smell," Spencer mutters. It'd been his idea, and he'd been proud of it till now.

Eddie blinks and seems to be at a loss for words. Scratching his head, he swats the Odor-Eaters away and glances down to the bag again. "It's all there?"

"Feels like it," T.J. says.

"Didn't ask you." Eddie turns his attention back to the group. "It's all there?"

"Yeah," Billy says.

"Liar," Eddie cocks the gun.

"It is, I swear," Spencer says, stepping forward. "We didn't take anything. We wanted to make as much…" he stops.

"You wanted to make as much money as possible, so you didn't dip into the merchandise, is that it?" Eddie asks.

Spencer stays silent. That and the fact the only one who wanted to smoke some of it was Carlos.

"Thing is, it ain't all here, is it?"

"The belt," Tori says.

Eddie moves the gun up and down. "Where is it?"

"It's back in our apartment. I didn't think there was a reason to bring it," Billy says.

"Not any reason? How about the fact that I was going to be here, you retard!" Eddie shouts, his free hand balled into a fist. The words echo in the locker room and cause everyone, including T.J. to flinch.

"I want my belt back," Eddie says. If it wasn't for the gun, Spencer would find how childish Eddie sounds to be funny.

Instead, the weapon makes this even more terrifying than ever.

"Give him back the belt, Billy," Carlos whispers, his head tilted up while blood flows from a cut on his lip.

"You heard Spencer, we don't have it," Billy says.

"But we'll give it to you," Tori says. "You want to pick it up right now? Let's go get it."

"And walk right into a trap like you four did? No way."

"Then we'll bring it to you," Billy says.

Narrowing his eyes, Eddie says, "Right. I just let you go and you guys will willingly give me the belt back. Like I'd buy that."

"Hey, Eddie?" T.J. speaks up, "We really should start wrapping things up. Mike said this place would only be clear for about fifteen minutes or so. What do you want to do?"

"I want the belt back. And I want all these fuckers to pay."

"That's a lot to ask for in," Carlos checks his watch, "five minutes."

Eddie keeps the gun trained on the group. When he speaks, he does so in a petulant kind of way, a child who is being forced to put away his toys and get ready for bath time. "Fine. You can bring the belt to me."

Spencer is about to breathe a sigh of relief when Eddie walks over to Tori and grabs her arm, "Till then, we're keeping her."

"Let go of me," Tori says, pulling her arm back.

"Let go of her," Billy moves towards Eddie, only for T.J. to step in between them.

"Yeah, you know what? This can work. You two," Eddie

says and motions to Billy and Eddie, "be at Woodland Terrace tomorrow at one. We'll do the trade then."

Spencer watches this play out, his eyes moving from Tori, to Billy, to Eddie. The inside of his stomach tightens, and he feels dizzy. "Take me," he says.

No one listens to him. Eddie is still dragging Tori away. Billy is shouting. Carlos lays on the ground.

"Take me!" He shouts. The two words are piled one after another, so that they come out as one single stream. But it causes Eddie to stop.

"Tori has the belt in her house. If you take her, we won't be able to get in and grab it. Take me instead."

Eddie cocks his head and smiles. "No."

CHAPTER FOURTEEN

SPENCER STARES AT THE GATES of Woodland Terrace, bouncing from one foot to the other wishing he'd been able to get something to eat beforehand. Though he doubts he'd be able to keep anything down, so maybe it's for the best.

"Let's call the cops, Billy," Spencer says, not caring how whiny his voice sounds.

"There's no reason to," his brother answers and readjusts the backpack on his shoulders.

Spencer laughs. "No reason to? Eddie threatened us with a gun. He beat the shit out of you and Carlos and took Tori. *Tori.*"

"He didn't beat the shit out me," Billy says. "And what would we tell them anyways? 'Yes, hello, officer? We stole from a drug dealer and now he's kidnapped my girlfriend, can you please help?'"

"We don't have to say all that. We could just tell them how Eddie went crazy and threatened us with a gun. That's probably enough."

"No," Billy says firmly. "We can handle this. Besides, you want Dad finding out about any of this? And if the cops get involved, that's it for RBWL. You don't want that, do you?"

Spencer says nothing. The truth is he hasn't thought about the Royal Brooks Wrestling League in a while. He can't even remember the last time he looked at his black notebook and tried to piece a new storyline or come up with a new gimmick for one of the wrestlers. Drug deals, kidnappings, and being held at gun point have taken priority the last few days.

"Look, it's that big retard."

Spencer squints to where his brother is looking and sees T.J. coming down the hill. He's dressed in a large black overcoat, which Spencer finds weird considering the sweltering heat.

"Please, Billy, let's just leave and call the cops, okay?"

"Too late, little brother."

The sound of the gate's motors grinding and turning presses against Spencer's spine and causes him to hold himself tight. T.J. stands on the other side of the gate, staring at the two brothers.

"You ready, Spencer? He asked for the two of us," Billy says.

I can do this, Spencer thinks and nods.

When the gate is open, T.J. turns around and begins walking back up the hill.

"I guess we're supposed to follow him," Spencer says.

Billy does just that. Spencer takes a deep breath and follows him.

"What did you tell Tori's parents?" Spencer asks in between puffs of breath as they climb up the inclined parking lot.

"Huh?" Billy asks.

"Tori's parents. Remember? I told you that you needed to call them and make up some lie about to why she wasn't coming home yesterday."

Billy stays quiet and keeps walking.

"You did call them, right, Billy?"

"I forgot, okay? It isn't like I didn't have enough to deal with. Shit, it took me half the night to convince Carlos and the rest of the guys not to do anything stupid and tag along."

Spencer closes his eyes and groans.

"We'll just make something up. She stayed at my place, or we went camping and forgot to tell them. It's no big deal, we done it before," he tells Billy. In a louder voice he says, "So, this is Woodland Terrace, huh? What a shit hole."

T.J. ignores Billy and takes a left by a row of mailboxes.

"Wait, that's not the way to Eddie's apartment," Spencer says.

"We're not going to Eddie's apartment," T.J. says without missing a step. They're moving in between apartment buildings, the sidewalk under their feet cracked and smudged with dirt and faded scuff marks. The sound of television and music bleeds out from apartment after apartment, punctuated with the occasional argument or loud videogame being played. The farther they move away from Eddie's apartment, the more times Spencer looks back and tries to retrace their steps. All the buildings look the same, and he swears this is the third time they've passed an abandoned tricycle.

"Where are you taking us?" Billy asks after another two minutes of walking.

Eddie ignores him.

"I asked you a question, asshole," Billy says and stops.

Spencer almost slams into him from behind.

T.J. turns and faces Billy. "You're lucky Eddie told me not to fuck you up."

"Big talk from someone who got beat by my little brother."

T.J.'s nostrils widen, his black eyebrows drawing together. "Once Eddie is done with you, then you and I can talk." He turns and starts walking again.

"Fuck," Billy says under his breath. "Least he could do is tell us where we're going."

Spencer is about to agree when he hears the cheers of a crowd and the sound of bodies hitting a mat. Sounds Spencer has grown up with. Spencer realizes where T.J. is taking them, and feels foolish for not figuring it sooner. It's just a few more minutes of walking before Spencer and Billy come face to face with Woodland Terrace's wrestling ring.

The ring is made up mostly of plywood, long strips of red carpet, and gray nylon ropes. Two of the ring posts are painted black, the ring platform only a few inches off the ground as opposed to the thirty-six inches Spencer knows a real wrestling ring should be. The longer he looks at the ring, the more details he notices are wrong. Instead of taut ropes providing just enough give to a wrestler bouncing off them, these ropes hang dangerously loose, with no protecting padding in three of the four corners. One of the posts is already sinking into the ground, causing the whole structure to tilt slightly to the left. There are no steps for wrestler's to climb into the ring, just a plastic stool.

A couple of chairs surround the ring, but most of the crowd—and there is a crowd—are standing. Spencer is surprised to see adults sprinkled among the teens in the crowd, some of them holding beer cans and looking like the exact sort of person who would be watching a group of teenagers put on a wrestling show in their backyard on a Sunday afternoon.

The crowd cheers when T.J, Billy, and Spencer step into the area. Billy and Spencer glance at each other as the cheers assault them. Someone throws a red cup at Spencer, yellow liquid splashing on his shoes. He doesn't have time to hope the liquid is Mountain Dew, T.J. stopping Billy and Spencer at the edge of the ring and saying, "Wait here." He then disappears into the crowd.

"I'm going to kill fucking Eddie," Billy says. "I really am."

Bad Religion's *Los Angeles is Burning* plays from the other side of the ring, and the crowd bursts into cheers, parting to let Eddie walk through.

He's in full wrestling regalia, wearing red and yellow tights and black wrestling boots which add two inches to his height. His mohawk stands at full attention, his chest glowing in the sun thanks to what Spencer imagines has to be three bottles of body oil. When Eddie slides into the ring, Spencer imagines he'll keep sliding and not be able to stop. Like T.J, Eddie too has an overcoat, the end of it dragging on the mat as he walks to each of the four corners of the ring and climbs the turn-buckles. Finishing posing for the crowd, Eddie walks over to the center of the ring and picks up the microphone. Tapping it, he winces at the screeching feedback and waits a few seconds before speaking into it. "Hello, WTF!"

The crowd cheers.

"You guys pumped for today, aren't you?" Eddie asks into the microphone. This elicits another cheer from the crowd. "And why wouldn't you? Not only do we have some kick ass matches for you, but like I promised in our last WTF video, I got a little show and tell for everyone here." Eddie points to the outside of the ring, where an old projector, like the ones teachers used to drag out and put overlays in middle school rest.

"But before we get to any of that, I want to introduce you guys to some special guests, who came all the way from the Royal Brooks apartments." With an overly telegraphed gesture, he motions to Billy and Spencer. The crowd attacks the brothers with jeers, paper cups, and insults, Eddie letting the crowd have their fun for a minute before speaking again.

"I'm going to tell you all a little story. It begins not too long ago, in a far off shit-stain called Royal Brooks." Eddie pauses to allow for boos. "Royal Brooks was a shitty little apartment complex which had a shitty little wrestling promotion, run by two shitty brother; a fat ass and a lover of sloppy seconds. These two brothers thought theirs was the little promotion that could, and God bless them did they try, putting on show after shitty show. But after a while, the two brothers real-ized what everyone else around them already knew. Their promotion, and their lives, sucked. So, you know what they tried to do? They tried to steal their way into better lives."

"Screw this," Billy says, moving towards ring.

Spencer grabs his wrist and stops. "Don't. He has Tori, remember?" he whispers to his brother.

Billy breathes through his nose but stays still.

"The two brothers, having at least an inch of good sense and taste, decided to steal from the best, and I think we all know who that is." Eddie stops and motions with his hands, the crowd chanting *Eddie, Eddie, Eddie*, on cue.

"I'll give the fat one credit, much as I hate to, guy actually managed to steal two very precious things from me." Now it's Billy's turn to grab Spencer, pulling him to the side just as a bottle crashes on the spot Spencer had been standing.

Eddie shakes his head. "I'll be honest with you. I was as disappointed with me as I was with the thief. But here's the thing they didn't realize and that you all know. When you go against Eddie Tornado, you better make sure to put me down!"

The crowd erupts into cheers and step closer the ring. Multiple hands push Spencer forward. They all work together to push Spencer towards the ring. Spencer turns to look at Billy, who is held back by the crowd. When he reaches the edge of the ring, Spencer has no other choice but to try to climb into it.

"Like a cow being led to slaughter, right, folks?" Eddie shouts. The crowd laughs.

After two failed attempts to climb the ring, Spence gives up and rolls under the bottom rope. He's just about to stand when Eddie moves closer and kicks him hard in the side.

Spencer's vision doubles as he crashes into the hard ring mat. He gasps for air, holding his ribs. Above him, he can just make out Eddie laughing over the cheers of the crowd.

"You didn't think you'd get out of this without some hurt, did you, boy?" Eddie asks, kicking him again.

Tears and sweat sting his eyes as Spencer tries again to stand up, only for Eddie to kick one of his arms away and send him crashing down back to the mat. Crouching next to him, Eddie pinches Spencer's cheek and whispers into the microphone. "Poor, baby. You tired of trying to hang with the big boys?"

"Leave him alone!" Billy shouts from outside the ring.

"I will," Eddie says. "In a second." Turning his attention back to Spencer he says, "Well? What do you say? Do you, in the immortal words of pussies everywhere, you give up?" he asks, jamming the microphone in Spencer's face.

Spencer tries to pull the words from wherever things like those are stored, but he can't find them He tries to tell himself saying the words will not only end the beating, but finish this thing and bring back Tori. But even so the words don't come out. Not even when Eddie starts prodding him with the microphone and making oinking sounds. Not even when Eddie gets up and starts kicking him again.

"What the fuck is going on here?"

The words are the cymbal falling on a stage. They silence the crowd, and stop Eddie mid kick. With the taste of bile and blood in his mouth, Spencer looks up and watches Eddie take a step back. His eyes are wide with something Spencer is intimately familiar with.

Fear.

Spencer turns to look at the direction Eddie's gaze is fixated on. At first his vision fights him, showing him nothing but blurred images, but it doesn't take long for them to solidify into human outlines, and then into someone he recognizes.

Tori stands next to a short, barrel chested man whom Spencer doesn't know. Her posture is rigid, one arm crossed over her chest while the other hangs limply from her side. She's staring down at the ground.

"Tori," Spencer hears Billy say.

"I asked a question," the man says. He never raises his voice, doesn't even move from the spot he's standing in, and yet there is a noticeable difference in the crowd's attitude. The thrall Eddie had them under is already dissipating, the ripple of indecision and confusion moving through the crowd and turning into a wave. Spencer can't help but note how almost everyone in the crowd does their best not to meet the man's eyes.

All but Eddie, who leans forward into the ring ropes and with a shake voice says, "Dad." Spencer laughs.

CHAPTER FIFTEEN

EDDIE'S DAD DOESN'T HAVE a mohawk.

It's an odd detail to focus on, but Spencer does so anyways, because it's one of the few things his tired and strained mind can grab hold of and not be in danger of short-circuiting. Instead Eddie's father keeps his hair closely cropped to his skull, highlighting ridges, bumps and scars. He's a short man with the built of a beer keg, muscled arms stretching the sleeves of the t-shirt he's wearing like tattooed trees breaking through the soil. Standing in the center of Woodland Terrace's wrestling ring, Eddie's dad reaches into the pocket of his jeans and pulls out a pack of cigarettes.

Spencer doesn't know much about Eddie's father, but the way he cut short the beating his son was giving him, end the entire show, and disperse the crowd with just a couple of words tells him he is someone everyone around here listens to.

Leaning awkwardly against one of the ring's corner post, Spencer's head rests against the middle turnbuckle pad. His entire body is sore, and there's a towel dabbed with blood on his lap. Eddie, Tori, and Billy stand only a couple of feet away, Eddie's father pacing back and forth in front of them. Other than the five of them inside the ring, there is no one else around. A tingle of worry courses through Spencer's spine.

"I'll ask again, what the fuck is going on here?" Eddie's father asks, pulling out a cigarette from a pack.

"Nothing, Dad," Eddie says, shifting from foot to foot, body oil dripping down and forming a stain on the mat. Next to him are Billy and Tori, looking like fishes ripped from their aquarium and put on a kitchen counter. Spencer wants to get up and go over to them, but his body refuses his orders and remains sitting on the mat.

"Nothing, Dad," Eddie's father mimics his son's words. "Bull. Shit. If nothing was going on, then I wouldn't have gotten a call from Mike telling me to haul my ass back here before my son did something stupid. Shit, boy, you just cost me five hundred bucks for an easy ass haul to Oklahoma."

Eddie looks down at the armrest. All the bravado, all the attitude he'd shown on every other occasion is gone, having retreated to some small and dark corner.

"I come home and find her," Eddie's father points to Tori, "tied up in the living room and my fucking piece gone. So I'm going to ask one last time, and for your sake, you better start talking, boy."

"They started it!" Eddie shouts, pointing to Tori. "She and those two stole our stash." His finger moves to accuse Billy, then Spencer. "I was just trying to make things right, Dad."

The man steps up to his son and smiles. With a smile still on his face he punches Eddie, sending him falling down into the mat to get tangled with the lower ring rope.

Billy and Tori move farther to the right side.

"How many times have I told you that the *stash* isn't yours?"

Wiping away the blood from his lip, Eddie doesn't meet his dad's glare. "Sorry, Dad."

"You're a kid, not some fucking drug dealer. Where the fuck is my gun?"

"In my room."

"Go get it. Now. And will you fucking change out of whatever gay shit you're wearing?"

Eddie rolls out of the ring. "Fucking kid," Eddie's father mutters, watching as his son takes a left and disappears behind a building. Digging into his pockets one more time, he asks, "Any of you three have a lighter?"

Spencer shakes his head and he thinks he hears Billy say a soft no.

"Fuck it," Eddie's father says, tossing the cigarette down to the floor. Turning his attention to Tori, he frowns.

"Didn't you use to live here?"

Tori nods.

"And you dated Eddie, right?"

Another nod.

Eddie's father grunts. "Always told him you were too hot to stick around. What's your name again, sweetheart?"

Spencer notices his brother tensing at Eddie's father's words. Tori must have too, because she reaches over and squeezes his hand. "Tori," she tells the Eddie's father.

"Tori. Maybe you can explain things to me. Is it true what my son said? Did you three steal my shit?"

"Not her," Billy speaks up. "Me and my brother. Ain't that right, Spencer?"

Spencer understands what his brother is doing. "Yeah. Me and Billy. We broke into your place, found the bag, and took it."

"Did you now?" Eddie's father looks down at Spencer. "And that's why my son was kicking the shit out of you?"

"And because he's an asshole." Spencer says without thinking.

Eddies father laughs and walks to Spencer, a grin on his face. "Isn't he?" Eddie's father says, leaning against the ring ropes and swiftly pressing his foot into Spencer's bruised side. Immediate pain radiates up and down Spencer's body, and he lets out a yell of pain.

"Stop it Mr. Travis!" Tori shouts. "They're lying, they didn't break into your house. I did."

"She's lying!" Spencer says, his body clenching through the pain.

With a sigh, Mr. Travis releases the pressure on Spencer's side and looks from at the three of them, his hands on his hips. Spencer thinks of his father, and he wonders if all parents end up adapting the same pose at some point or another. Suddenly, all he wants to do is go home.

"Getting real sick and tired of all the lies here. Let's see if I can sparse some shit out. You all," Mr. Travis motions to the Billy, Tori, and Spencer, "or one of you three, or two of you three, you stole my weed, right?"

No one speaks. Mr. Travis glances at them and steps forward, his hand shooting out and grabbing Billy by the throat. "Yes. Or no."

"Yes," Tori says, trying to pull Mr. Travis's arm away.

"But we didn't mean to," adds Spencer.

"Oh, well, if you didn't mean to," Mr. Travis says, pulling his hand back. Billy gasps and sucks in a lungful of air. "I guess that's all that matters then."

"We didn't know we took it, we swear. We were looking for something else," Spencer says and tries to get up, only for the pain to be too much. He slumps back against the post.

"What were you looking for?" Mr. Travis asks.

Again, there's silence. As much as Spencer wants this to be over, he can't bring himself to reveal the reason why all this started. Tori, on the other hand doesn't seem to have any qualms about it.

"Photos of me that your son took. Private photos which he said he was going to show to everyone."

"Shit, really?" Mr. Travis says, and Spencer swears he hears a touch of pride in his voice.

"We just wanted the photos back," Tori continues

"Explain to me how photos and my weed look alike, then," Mr. Travis says.

"Don't listen to them," Eddie says. He's back and changed from his wrestling gear and into a pair of sweatpants and shirt. He steps inside the ring, the gun is held in his right hand. "All that matters is that they stole *your* weed and *my* belt. And then they tried to sell the weed back to Mike. Probably to use the money and try to make their shitty wrestling promotion more like mine."

"I knew it," Eddie's father says, turning to look at his son. "I fucking knew it." He looks at Eddie, shaking his head. "This ain't for some slut photos. It's all because of your stupid wrestling thing, ain't it? Christ, it's not enough that you look like a goddamn homo grabbing your friends around, or the fuck-load of calls I've gotten over this stupid ring I let you set up. Now it's fucking my business."

"I was just trying to—"

"That's the thing with you Eddie. You never try. You just fuck up. I want all this," he stops and motions around him, "Gone by tomorrow. Now give me the gun before you shoot yourself."

"But Dad—"

"Give me the gun, Eddie." Mr. Travis steps towards his son.

Eddie glances down at the gun on his hand and then raises it, pointing it at his father. "No."

Eddie's father blinks. "Give me the fucking gun."

"No!" Eddie shouts. "I'll fix this, Dad." He swivels his aim so that it's pointing to Billy. "I'll show everyone not to mess with the Travis men."

Billy stays frozen, his eyes glued to the gun. He opens his mouth, as if to say something, but nothing comes out. "Eddie, please don't do this," Tori whispers.

"You guys shouldn't have stole from us." Eddie's voice cracks, but the gun doesn't waver.

"You can have your belt back," Spencer says. Unzipping the backpack which is by his feet, he reaches in and pulls out the Woodland Terrace belt. "See?" he says.

"It's too late," Eddie says. "We have to teach you a lesson about what happens when you mess with us, right Dad?"

"Quit fucking around and give me the gun, Eddie. That's the last time I ask."

"I'm not fucking around!" Eddie shouts, turning to point the gun at his dad. "I'm making things right."

Mr. Travis stands perfectly still. "Okay, okay, I get it, you're making things right."

"And I'm not a screw up. And wrestling isn't gay!" Eddie shouts. "Now who's going to get it first? Should it be Billy? Maybe Tori? Or you, Spencer?"

Spencer holds the wrestling belt in his hand as the gun is aimed at him. "Please just let us go, Eddie. You have everything back now."

"Too late for that," Eddie says. His eyes are bloodshot.

Do something. Do something. Spencer shouts to his limbs, attempting to will them into action. But his limbs, are hypnotized by the gun pointed at him. He can't even bring himself to cry.

It's Tori who ends up doing something. She throws herself at Eddie, the two tumbling down to the mat, the gun slipping out of Eddie's hand. Billy takes Tori's cue runs at Eddie's father.

Unlike his son, Mr. Travis sees the attack coming and readies himself. He waits until Billy is almost on him, feints to the left and throws a right hook which lands on Billy's forehead. Spencer brother reels back and crumples down to the mat.

"Fucking kids," Mr. Travis says, walking towards Tori and Eddie, who continue to struggle on the floor. "I'm done with this shit." He bends down to pick the gun up.

DO SOMETHING. The neurons in Spencer's brain kick-start his body and he's able to stand, though not without every part of his body screaming in pain. Continuing to hold on to the wrestling belt, and in unsteady legs, Spencer walks over to Eddie's father, who is just standing up, gun in his hand. He's points it at Billy just as Spencer lets out a yell and runs at him. The yell vibrates in his throat, packed with all the frustration, jealousy, and anger he's been holding onto, and it catches Mr. Travis' attention. He swivels and turns towards Spencer, just as Spencer grips the belt by its end and swings it as hard as he can.

The sound the belt makes when it connects with Mr. Travis's face is louder than Spencer expected, louder than when it happens in televised wrestling. Mr. Travis also doesn't go down as fast as they do in television either. He takes a step to the left and wavers, blood trickling from his forehead. Raising the gun, it looks like he's going to pull the trigger when Spencer swings the belt again, hitting him on the other side of the head. The sound is even louder than before, the jolt of the belt almost throwing Spencer off balance.

Eddie's father goes down to the floor.

Billy is back on his feet and runs to Tori, who is still rolling on the floor with Eddie. Before he can reach her, Tori grabs Eddie's mohawk with both hands and knees him in the groin. Eddie lets out a cry, sliding away from her while holding his groin.

Spencer is still trying to catch his breath. He's exhausted, all the adrenaline which carried him up from the recliner now gone, replaced with an aching so deep he wants to cry. His whole body hurts so much, and the ring won't stop spinning. But he smiles. Because he did something good, something brave. Something for himself. The belt is still in his hand, but it's getting heavier and heavier by the second, so he drops it.

"Spencer, you're bleeding."

Billy is helping Tori up from the floor when she says this. Spencer wants to smile and tell her he's been bleeding for most of the day, but he's so damned *tired*.

The mat looks so inviting. Like an island of rest. Spencer tries to take a step towards only to find the entire ring tilting at an angle. Blinking, he glances at Tori and Billy, finding only blurred figures at the edge of his vision. Another blink, and for the first time he feels the wetness on his side. Shaky fingers move to his right side, where his shirt feels stickier than usual. He knows it before his fingertips land on the dampness, before he brings them back up to his face and sees them stained with red.

"Help." The word is slurred, and he isn't even sure it fully comes out. His knees buckle under him and Spencer falls to the ground. "Help," he says again. He's crying, the tears running down his cheeks.

"Spencer, Spencer." His brother is next to him. "Call 9-1-1, Tori!" he hears Billy shout. "Come on, Billy, hang on. Shit, I'm sorry, I'm sorry I was a shitty brother." Billy is crying. Spencer can't remember the last time his brother cried. When their mother left. Spencer wants to tell him that he wasn't a shitty brother, but he doesn't, because he doesn't think he should be lying when he's about to die. That probably gets you banned from heaven automatically. He settles on telling Billy, "you weren't always shitty." Which is the truth.

Spencer closes his eyes and waits for the pin count.

CHAPTER SIXTEEN

HOSPITAL FOOD SUCKS.

Spencer pushes away the half-eaten tray of food and sighs. What he wouldn't give for the cheeseburger Carlos told him he would sneak in the next time he came to visit.

He hears a knock on his door, and looks up just in time to see Billy and Tori walk into the room.

Billy is still sporting the shiner he got from Mr. Travis, but otherwise looks just like always. Tori has her hair braided and is wearing a red summer dress which stands out in the sterile, white hospital room. Spencer glances to the machines he's hooked up to, wondering if they'll start beeping and going crazy like they would on a cartoon. But no, they just keep with their constant beep he's learned to fall asleep to.

"Hey, Spence, how you holding up?" Billy asks. "Good," Spencer answers. "Starving, but good."

Picking up the gelatin off his tray, Billy plops down on the chair next to Spencer's bed. "Look on the bright side. You already look thinner. A couple more weeks here and you'll be a changed man."

"Billy!" Tori says.

"What? That'd be a good thing." Billy says in between mouthfuls of gelatin.

"Seriously, Spencer, you doing alright?" Tori asks him.

He nods. "As good as a guy can shot can be."

"Count yourself lucky, bro. At least you're not home with Dad. The guy hasn't left me out of his sight in days.

And when he's not around, he continuously checks up with me. Even when I'm at work."

Billy had gotten an offer from Dairy Queen a day after Spencer was admitted to the hospital. The only reason their dad was allowing Billy to keep the job was because it made easier to check up on him. That, and all the money was being put away for college. Or a defense fund, depending on how things went.

"He's waiting outside, by the way."

"He's been doing okay?" Spencer asks.

"Surprisingly, yeah."

"What about your parents, Tori?"

"They're taking things like you'd expect them to take. We're umm, moving from Royal Brooks."

Spencer sits up on his bed "Wait, what? You can't. Why?"

"It's okay, Spencer, relax," Tori says. "We're moving because they think this guy," she points to Billy, "is a bad influence. Well, that and the rent increase."

"Where are you moving to?"

"Oh, he's going to love this," Billy says.

"They're thinking Woodland Terrace."

Spencer stares at Tori with his mouth open.

Tori shrugs. "They have good move in specials, apparently. And with Eddie and his dad gone from there, they figure it'll be okay."

"But what about everyone else? All the WTF guys? T.J.? You won't be safe there!" Spencer says.

"Most of the WTF guys had no idea what was happening apparently. They were just in it to have fun and wrestle, like our guys."

"And the word is the big retard is off in juvie for a while."

"With Eddie?" Spencer asks.

"Nah, Eddie is supposedly in a group home somewhere. Considering his dad, no wonder he was the way he was."

"Yeah."

"Oh hey, we brought you some entertainment," Tori said, reaching into her bag.

"Dad said this place doesn't get wrestling, so we figured you'd probably be missing it."

Tori hands Spencer a couple of wrestling DVD, two magazines, a couple of books from the library, and his portable game system. Spencer glances down to them and then smiles and Tori and Billy. "Thanks."

The three of them are silent for a minute. Billy clears his throat and punches Spencer on the shoulder and says, "Anyways, you probably need your rest or whatever. Do you know how much longer you're going to be stuck in here? RBWL needs you, man."

"I dunno, ask Dad. The doctors tell him everything."

"Okay. We'll stop by later this week and see how you're doing." Billy gets up from his seat and starts walking to the door. He motions for Tori to follow him.

"Just a sec, Billy. I wanted to talk to Spencer. Can you give me a second?"

Billy frowns but nods. "Alright, I'll be by the vending machines."

When he's gone, Tori grins and whispers, "He's been eating a lot of candy lately. And exercising less."

"You should tell him something. He's going to hate himself if he gains all the weight back."

"I will. But he's stressed enough as it is. He was really worried about you, Spencer. We all were." She puts her hand on his and squeezes. "Seeing you lying on the floor, bleeding," her voice quivers as she continues, "I'm sorry, Spencer. So sorry. This is all my fault. If I hadn't gone to you because of the photos—"

"The photos! We never got them,"

"Who cares about the photos. I'm sure they're at the land-fill somewhere after the Woodland Terrace's landlord cleaned out Eddie's apartment."

"Still. We should have tried to get them when we were there."

"Damn it, Spencer!" Tori says and squeezes his hand harder. "Stop. You can't keep doing this. To me or yourself."

Spencer's mouth goes dry. He pulls his hand away from Tori's. "What are you talking about?"

"This, Spencer," Tori says. "You and me. It's not your fault. I know how you see me, and I think… I didn't mean to, but I think I took advantage of that. I'm sorry."

"Why are you saying this?" Spencer asks.

"Because I want to be your friend, not your crush."

Being shot didn't hurt as much as this. Tori reaches for his hand again, and it takes everything in Spencer's powers not to recoil at her touch, not to tell her to leave. He looks away from Tori, his eyes falling on the wrestling magazines she and Billy brought him. Seeing the cover reminds Spencer of the Woodland Terrace ring, of the way Eddie crowed about it and WTF, of his entire life, and how it was all just a gimmick—a delusion.

Spencer doesn't want to be Eddie.

He reaches for Tori's hand and gives her a smile.

"I want that too."

Tori wipes away her tear and hugs him. After a brief hesitation, Spencer hugs her back.

She leaves a few minutes later, and like Billy, promises to visit later this week.

As he waits for his father to come into the room, he flips through the wrestling magazines and stops on a picture of a wrestler his face covered a crimson mask of blood. *Richard Romero bleeding the hardway after a chair shot to the head* the caption reads. Spencer stares at the picture for a long time, before closing the magazine and putting it atop the food tray. He leans his head back and stares up the ceiling.

He wishes he had his black notebook with him.

ACKNOWLEDGMENTS

This book would not exist without Ron Phillips and the team at Shotgun Honey. My very first published story was via his great flash fiction and he's always been a supportive presence not only to me, but to all crime authors and readers. I promise Thursday Malone is on the way, Ron!

I would also like to thank my entire family for their love and support. My dad for taking me to my first lucha show, and my mom for surprising me with random books while growing up. I am the person I am now because of them, gracias.

To all the fine folks on Twitter who have inspired me, encouraged me, and kept me sane. If this book is any good, it's because I'm trying to keep up with writers like Dave White, Angel Colon, Todd Robinson, Thomas Pluck, Chuck Wendig, Alex Segura, Gabino Iglesias, Chris Irvin, Rob Hart, and so many more.

To Scott Keith and his blog and everyone at the Penny Arcade forum for making the wrestling product entertaining even during Roman Reign's world title reign. And to every wrestler which has made me jump out of my chair and cheer till my throat was raw.

And finally to you, reader. For giving this book a chance. I hope it was more fun than a chair to the head.

HECTOR ACOSTA's short stories have appeared in *Weird Noir*, *Thuglit*, and all three volumes of *Shotgun Honey Anthologies*. *Hardway* is his first novella. He lives in New York with his wife and dog, and is working on his next book. He's 99% sure wrestling is scripted, and can be followed on Twitter @ hexican.

ABOUT SHOTGUN HONEY BOOKS

Thank you for reading *HARDWAY* by Hector Acosta.

Shotgun Honey began as a crime genre flash fiction webzine in 2011 created as a venue for new and established writers to experiment in the confines of a mere 700 words. More than a decade later, Shotgun Honey still challenges writers with that storytelling task, but also provides opportunities to expand beyond through our book imprint and has since published anthologies, collections, novellas and novels by new and emerging authors.

We hope you have enjoyed this book. That you will share your experience, review and rate this title positively on your favorite book review sites and with your social media family and friends.